A House Without Windows

By

Stevie Turner

A House Without Windows

Thanks to Libbie Grant and also Obsessed by Books Designs for the cover, and my gratitude goes to Enid Blyton for writing the Island of Adventure and starting me out on my love of reading all those years ago.

Also thanks to Caleb Clayton for formatting my manuscript.

Dedication

Dedicated to all those rescued from captivity.

Synopsis

Newly-pregnant Dr Beth Nichols is happily engaged to Liam Darrah, a fellow doctor. She has no idea she is being stalked by ex-patient Edwin Evans as she makes her way home one evening after a late shift at the hospital. After being anaesthetised she wakes up in Edwin's basement, held against her will, and eventually gives birth there without medical help. However, Beth tries to stay positive, and somehow knows that Liam will still be out there searching for her. Every night she lies awake and looks up at the light bulb that is never switched off, and prays that one day they will be together again.

Table of Contents

PROLOGUE

THE UNPREPOSSESSING EXTERIOR of the suburban 1930's end-of-terrace house was giving nothing away. Inspector John Hatton pushed past the usual group of ghouls and rubberneckers, dipped his slightly overweight body under the cordon, and opened the gate leading to the tidy pocket-handkerchief front garden.

"Morning Ford."

"Morning Sir."

"You get all the best jobs don't you? Anyone in or out?"

"Not as far as I know, Sir."

"Have you had a word with the neighbours?"

"The ones I've spoken to say he was always a bit of a loner; kept himself to himself. They don't really know much about him."

Stamping his feet as he sheltered from the January chill in the half–enclosed front porch, Ford looked to Hatton as though he was freezing his arse off. Hatton let a faint smile play around his lips as he realised that yes, this morning there *was* actually somebody worse off than him.

He curbed the impulse to wipe his feet on the welcome mat just inside the front door. Grimacing at the irony, he put on plastic overshoes and gloves and continued down the hallway into the kitchen.

Everything was still in its place, modern and clean. The door to the dishwasher was open as though it had been in the process of being emptied; there were still clean plates, bowls, and pots and pans stacked neatly. Knives, forks and spoons filled the cutlery compartment, all with their handles facing the same way. Hatton noticed the five large plastic containers still standing side by side above the dishwasher on the work-top, each full to the brim with a different breakfast cereal.

He could imagine guests (if there had ever been any) popping into the kitchen for a drink of water and wondering why somebody living on his own would have wanted to buy so many containers of cereal, and why they would have required such a huge American walk-in fridge. He opened the fridge door that stood next to the dishwasher; there were seven pints of full-fat milk in the storage space in the door, three large portions of raw fillet steak on the bottom shelf, and numerous types of vegetables, salad stuff and fruits filling the middle two. Various yoghurts sat on the top shelf in regimented lines, segregated into flavours, with the ones nearest their sell-by date at the front. Twelve raw eggs sat in holders slightly too small for them in the door above the milk.

Hatton took one last glance at the food that would soon begin to spoil; *he could have just eaten that fillet steak with some chips, mushrooms and peas.*

Walking around the central table he noticed the dishcloth folded neatly on the draining board, not just thrown down as he would have done. He opened the cupboards underneath the sink; bleach, Dettol, and washing-up liquid stood one behind the other on the left side, next to two large packets of sanitary towels on the right.

The guests would have really begun to wonder at the sight of those…..

He sighed and closed the cupboard and looked around some more. Adjacent to the sink stood a washing machine still full of damp women's clothing, and on the far wall was a long clean-looking worktop with cupboards underneath containing sweets and crisps, and what looked like a pantry just outside the kitchen door. Hatton checked inside and found shelves overflowing with rice, spaghetti, pasta, potatoes, more tinned food, and the door to what resembled yet another American type of walk-in-fridge, silver in colour, but built into a recess with a bolt on the outside. The bolt was pulled back into the open position, and the door was slightly ajar. He walked towards it, opened the door fully, and trod carefully down the narrow flight of steps.

He had to see it just once more, before the house was bulldozed and razed to the ground.

CHAPTER 1 - BETH

THE BILE TASTED bitter in my mouth. I did not need to call upon my six years of medical training to realise that the symptoms of amenorrhea combined with morning sickness and aching breasts were sufficient to tell me that I was probably pregnant. I lifted my head up from the toilet bowl and was glad that Liam was working nights this week. I would not want him to see me like this. Our paths would be cross-ing later that morning, but by then I knew I would be rav-enous again and he would not suspect a thing. As I cleaned my teeth I decided to ask Mona, my new A&E colleague, to take some blood for an HCG; I wanted to be certain.

The alarm would not go off for another two hours. I climbed back into bed, but could not settle down. The thought of a new little life growing inside me was enough to banish all sleep from my brain, and I ached to tell Liam the news. I twisted the engagement ring around on my finger, willing the hours to pass until I saw him again around 09:30. Eventually I gave up, got out of bed and took a shower. By the time I had dried my hair I was feeling much better.

He crashed through the door of our accommodation unit, dog tired. Nights did not agree with him; I think it had some strange effect on his alimentary canal. He always felt nauseated until he managed to eat some breakfast.

"Hi! Busy night?"

I put my arms around him; he smelt of sweat, antiseptic and weariness. I knew I would be giving out the same odour by 10pm when my shift ended. He sighed and yawned simultaneously.

"Nicky was off sick again. There was just Isaac, me and three nurses. Thank God it wasn't a Friday night, eh?"

He kissed me and I enjoyed the all-too-brief feeling of his arms around me. Standing there together in our little room I wanted time to stand still. Unsure as to whether my sudden fear at losing him was due to my possible delicate condition or just a vague worry that he might find somebody else one day, I held him tighter than usual.

"Are you okay, Beth?"

He cupped my chin with his hand and I lifted my face to look up at him.

"I just missed waking up with you, that's all." I smiled.

"Same here." He yawned again. "What's to eat?"

"Beans on toast, or boiled eggs."   I could not stomach frying rashers of bacon at that precise moment.

"Just some toast for now. I can't eat much. I'm going to have a shower and then hit the sack."

He wriggled out of my embrace and headed for the bathroom, divesting himself of his clothing along the way. The urge to pick them up and put them in the laundry basket was overwhelming, but I was not going to start doing the same thing as my mother had done for over 30 years of married life. I left them where they lay; a soiled trail, a testament to my hard-working but rather laid-back fiancée.

I smiled at Liam, as wrapped in my towelling robe and still damp from his shower, he came and stood behind me as I fed slices of bread into the toaster. I turned and buried my face in his chest, inhaling a pleasant aroma of shower gel.

"Mmmm......you smell lovely. I wish I didn't have to go to work later. We could stay in bed all day"

"Working nights sucks big time." He smoothed my long hair with his hands and kissed the top of my head.

"At least you'll get next week off." I wrapped my arms around his waist. "I love you."

"And I love *you*. Come and eat some toast in bed with me."

How could I resist? The toast was thick and buttery, and our unmade bed suddenly looked rather inviting now that Liam had divested himself of my robe and was climbing naked under the sheet. Giggling like two naughty teenagers caught having sex by an irate parent, I set the alarm for 1pm, piled a plate high with toast, and mindful of crumbs, we ate close together over a tray and sipped hot, sweet tea. Hunger pangs catered for, we then made slow delicious love, savouring each other's bodies as though it was the last day on earth. Sated, we fell asleep in each other's arms.

Goodness knows how Liam could have slept through the radio alarm blasting out 'Layla', but he did. I rose up like a startled fawn and re-set it for Liam, momentarily angry that our peace had been shattered. Showering again and dressing quickly, I grabbed a sandwich and a cup of coffee, checked that my bleep and badge were in my bag, and scribbled a heart on a post-it with our names inside, leaving it on my pillow for Liam to find.

It was a five minute walk to the Accident & Emergency department. The warm May afternoon held a promise of summer days to come, and I sauntered happily along the hospital paths enjoying the fresh air. As always I wondered what would be waiting for me in A&E when I got there. Unlike Liam I enjoyed the drama. Liam favoured paediatrics, but I liked the challenge of making an on-the-spot diagnosis. I really could not see myself working in any other speciality.

What with the ruptured appendix, the gallstones, the WPW Syndrome, numerous fractured limbs, and trying to communicate with dazed geriatrics, my intention to ask for an HCG test eventually remained unrequested. It was only at 22:15 when I left the hospital to walk home that I remembered I had not had a chance to speak to Mona. I made a mental note to rectify this the following day.

The hospital grounds were quiet, apart from the sound of a car's engine. I walked along, happily thinking about what our baby might look like. I recognised the face as he drove up beside me and opened the passenger window. The drug addict was asking for directions to A&E again. I had found him overtly licentious when I had treated him previously for pain, haematuria and withdrawal. If I had not stepped back from the trolley he was lying on at the time he would have reached up and touched my hair, so enamoured was he of my long blonde ponytail.

I tried to think of his name, but it escaped me. There was a strong smell of aftershave. I had to lean in to make eye contact, but remember nothing more after that.

CHAPTER 2 - BETH

MY HEAD IS pounding, and a bright light above ensures I quickly have to close my eyes again. Feeling nauseated, I lie still, using my other senses to try and recognise sounds or a particular aroma which could confirm to me that I am still in the accommodation unit. However, I can hear nothing at all; not even the usual birdsong, and there is an unaccountably earthy, damp smell. Suddenly curious, I fight sickness and confusion to sit up and take note of my surroundings.

I have no idea where I am. I am lying on top of a double bed. It is not the bed where I wrap myself contentedly around Liam. There is a duvet beneath me covered with a surprisingly clean-looking lilac flowery cover, which is complete with matching sheets and pillow cases. There does not seem to be any other furniture. There are no windows, and the bare bulb above my head is the only source of light.

Slightly panicky now and ignoring the increased hammering in my brain, I stand up shakily on the cold, concrete floor. The room is quite small, and I reach the only visible door after taking just a few steps. It is not the sort of door that I could break down. I turn the handle, but it refuses to yield.

I am locked in. I want to scream in fright, but stop myself at the last moment from sliding into rampant hysteria. I reason that whoever is keeping me in the room against my will would not want me making too much noise which might alert searchers to my location. I figure that I need to keep on the right side of my captor.

I take a few paces past the bed to the other side, towards where the wall finishes, and I look around the corner. There is a toilet and one sink in a tiny bathroom which is devoid of both windows and doors. To the left of the sink I spot a rail containing a matching towel and flannel. In the middle of the taps lies a new bar of soap. There is an unused cup inside the sink, still in some sort of plastic wrapping.

My mouth is dry, and I realise I am terribly thirsty. I tear off the cup's wrapping and fill it with water from the tap. The cold liquid is manna from heaven. I can even imagine the action of peristalsis, as the water trickles down my parched throat to my stomach. The nausea begins to recede, although my head is still sore.

I do not know what the time is or if it is still Wednesday 20th May. The dearth of windows ensures not only the absence of another escape route, but also reinforces the certainty that I have no knowledge as to whether it is day or night.

I run some hot water into the sink to wash my face. The water gurgles in the naked copper pipes running up the wall, making me wonder if the sound is going to alert anybody to the fact that I am awake.

I am correct. Within a few moments I can hear the sound of keys turning in the distance, heavy footsteps approaching, and then a bolt being pulled back on the door to my room and another key rattling in the lock.

I walk forward and face my captor. With dismay I see he is the drug addict I treated a few weeks previously, and the one who pulled up beside me in his car to ask for directions as I walked home. Was that yesterday? He looks around forty years of age; there are flecks of grey in his dark hair and beard, and he is carrying a tray piled high with sandwiches and fruit. Over his arm is draped a selection of underwear and clothes, which I presume are for me, as all I have are the clothes I am wearing. For several moments neither of us say anything. I look beyond him to the open door, judging as to whether I could dart past him and make a break for freedom. As though he could read my thoughts he closes the door and locks it from the inside, balancing the tray on one hand, and then comes over towards the bed.

I edge around the other side of the bed away from him. He places the tray and the clothes down upon the bed, and backs off towards the door. We stand there, silently sizing each other up like two prize-fighters. I ask him what day it is, but he does not reply. He then turns around and goes out, locking the door behind him.

I decide to give up asking him for the date and time. It is easy to decipher the approximate hour if I look at the offer-ings on the tray. Over the following days I see that there is always egg, bacon, mushrooms and tomatoes, or a hot meal and sandwiches. Sometimes the latter two will arrive together and he does not come down for the rest of the day, so I assume that he has a job of some kind. Any dirty clothes or food I leave he removes when he brings me the next meal. Regular clean clothes and towels arrive that harbour an aroma of lavender conditioner. One day I feel brave and inform him that I do not like mushrooms, and to my surprise these are replaced at the next visit with baked beans.

Many trays are delivered before he utters even one word to me. I have ceased asking when I can be released, and just sit placidly on the bed when I hear his footsteps. One day he brings me a piece of fillet steak, a tomato, some chips, and a cup of tea.

"Thank you." I pull the tray onto my lap and begin to eat.

"You're welcome. My name is Edwin."

"I'm Beth."

"I know. When you need those lady things, tell me and I'll get them for you."

His voice is deep and resonant. I mask my surprise at hearing him speak, particularly about sanitary towels, and just concentrate on eating. My baby requires nourishment, and must be fed. However, he does not back off this time but stands watching me, a slightly lascivious expression on his face. I begin to inwardly panic, as this is out of the ordinary. When I finish the meal my heart is racing uncontrollably, and I have broken out in a hot sweat.

"Take your clothes off."

He is broad and muscular; there is no way that I can fight back. With a sinking feeling akin to dread I know what is going to happen next. He unzips his trousers, and I can already see an erection through his underpants.

My breasts are swollen with pregnancy hormones, but my abdomen is still flat enough so as not to cause suspicion. When he lies on top of me I focus my mind on Liam; the ripe corn colour of his hair, and most of all his sensual smile. I know he will never stop searching for me, and I try to imagine the day when we can be reunited.

Thankfully Edwin only cares for his own personal gratification. Compared to Liam I would say that Edwin's gauche, inexperienced performance of the sexual act marks him out as virginal.

There are no words exchanged. His semen leaks out onto the bed as he pulls out of me and dresses quickly. When he takes my tray back upstairs and locks the door, I run to the toilet and vomit all the fillet steak and chips back up.

Unfortunately it is not long before sex becomes a regular part of his routine. I can always tell by the look on his face if I am to be subjected to more abuse, and so I become adept at focusing my thoughts on Liam until the ordeal is over. I start to plait my hair so as not to leave it hanging down my back. After approximately four months of incarceration he notices that my abdomen has started to swell.

"I'm pregnant." I tell him, whilst sitting naked on the edge of the bed hugging my aching breasts.

"Fuck." He looks at my stomach as he dresses himself.

"If you don't want any more children you will need to use condoms after the birth." I look at him, inwardly dreading the thought of ever conceiving his child.

"Is it mine?" He shakes his head.

"Of course it is." I pull on a top. "Who else has there been but you?"

"I'm going to be a father?" He looks at me astoundingly.

I nod, and for a second I think he seems pleased at the fact.

He swallows the lie. In fact he seems remarkably un-worldly regarding matters concerning the female reproductive system, not even enquiring why I have had no need of 'lady things' since the beginning of my incarceration. I have come to the conclusion that I am definitely the first woman he has ever performed the sex act on. I begin to wonder if indeed, he has ever had a girlfriend at all.

I take his naivety one step further. Putting on my grav-est doctor's voice I inform him that sex during pregnancy would probably be harmful to his baby. He nods seriously, and to my utter astonishment and delight the daily abuse stops. I hug myself with joy at the thought of being left alone for the foreseeable future.

I start to push my luck, and complain I am bored. He apolo-gises that he totally forgot about providing things to keep me occupied. I tell him I would like to knit some baby clothes, and he brings wool, knitting needles and patterns. I stick my neck out further and ask for some newspapers, but am met with stony silence. However, he brings some cheap women's magazines, the kind where degraded and abused women tell their stories to equally downtrodden female readers. It is only when I am halfway through one of the magazines that I real-ise I am now in the same unfortunate position.

I am learning to endure. I know it is not worth fighting him to try and escape. There is no way out. I know that Liam will find me one day. I have to stay positive. I knit fu-riously; Liam's baby will be well-clothed. I construct matinee coats, bootees, trousers and hats. I nestle a hat and coat in the crook of my arm and rock it backwards and forwards lovingly.

I must ensure my musculature does not deteriorate in the confines of my prison. Every day when I wake up I now perform the Pilates exercises I often suggested to angry patients who would have benefited from them, but who I knew would ignore my advice and keep looking for that elusive miracle cure. I take my time and try to keep my body in the best possible shape for the impending birth.

I ask Edwin where I will give birth. He tells me I am a doctor, so I can deliver the baby myself on the bed. I should be seeing a midwife now for check- ups and blood tests. There will be none. I hope fervently there will be no complications.

The months roll past. I send thought messages to Liam and tell him he is going to be a father. I knit a whole wardrobe for the baby, and prepare a list of things I will need. Thank-fully Edwin agrees to my requests for a plastic sheet, sanitary towels, and extra towels and nappies. He has even given me a ball of string and a small pair of scissors when I tell him I will need something with which to cut and tie off the umbili-cal cord. The scissors are not overly sharp, but they will have to do.

I am as ready as I can be for the birth. I am too big to do any exercises now, and so just spend my days knitting and waiting. I have seen women in childbirth during the weeks of obstetrics training, and I pray to God that I can cope with the pain without analgesia.

I am having a wash at the sink when I feel the waters breaking. Edwin left me some sandwiches with my breakfast tray, and so I know he has gone to work. I quell a rising panic and sit on the toilet until the rush of water has passed. I finish washing and put my nightdress back on instead of day clothing.

Within a short time the first contractions begin. I relax upon the bed because it seems that the pains are within my capabilities to endure. I can feel my abdomen tightening with each contraction, and the baby kicking, eager to get out of its prison. I feel like telling it to stay in there; the prison it is coming into is not much improved on the one it is leaving.

The pains increase. I have no way of measuring time, and so have no idea how long I have been in labour. I am hungry, but eschew the sandwiches wrapped in cling film. From what I have seen of women in labour, whatever they have eaten tends to come back up again.

I stand up and hope that gravity will aid the baby's expulsion from my womb. I start to pace the floor, stopping to let each contraction take its course. I can walk nine steps before I have to turn around and go the other way. I try not to think how two of us will cope in such a tiny space.

The labour drags on interminably. I sip water to stay hydrated. The pains are making me sweat, and my nightdress is soaking wet. I am tired with all the pacing, and focus on placing the plastic sheeting over the duvet. I cover the sheet with towels, and lay on my side on the bed next to the scissors and string. The pain makes me want to cry, but I need to endure silently and not panic. I must be in control of my emotions in order to bring Liam's baby safely into the world.

The focusing on an object does not work. I smile wryly to myself and wonder how many times I told labouring women to do the same. It did not seem to work for them either. Finally I scream at the cold concrete walls, efficient as always at dulling any sound. Nobody comes to my aid.

At last I feel an urge to open my bowels, and I know this is the last phase of childbirth. I brace my back against the bedhead, grab my knees, and push with all my might. My hand can feel the baby's head presenting in the birth canal. I wait for another contraction and push again. I scream with pain as another contraction tears through my body, and give another push that threatens to almost stop my heart.

The shoulders are out. One last push and I have my baby girl. Her lungs are wonderfully efficient, and she turns from purple to pink. She is alive. My ordeal is almost over. All that is left is to massage the fundus to encourage it to contract and expel the placenta. One last contraction and push, and the placenta lies on the plastic sheet. When the umbilical cord stops pulsing I tie it off with string close to the baby, and then a few inches further down, and then cut it in the middle of the tied section with the scissors. My baby is a separate entity; there are now two of us in prison.

Clutching the baby I wash us, pad myself up, dress the baby, and tie the placenta and bloodied towels up in the plastic sheet for Edwin to burn. I lay down and put the baby to my breast, who I can see will look the image of Liam. I celebrate the birth by eating all four of Edwin's ham and tomato sandwiches.

CHAPTER 3 - AMY

MUMMY WONDERS IF it will be Christmas soon, but I don't know what she means. She says that when she was a little girl she would get lots of presents on Christmas Day, and there would be a big tree in her house with lots of twinkling fairy lights on the branches and shiny baubles that she could see her reflection in. I've never seen a tree, so Mummy drew one for me in my colouring book and showed me. I don't understand why there was a tree in her house.

My name is Amy, and Mummy thinks I must be about eight or nine years old because my big front teeth are growing in. I have long blonde hair like Mummy that I can sit on. Mummy puts it in a plait and she showed me how to plait hers, and she taught me how to read. She says I can read and write really well, and I like writing stories. I write everything down in a secret diary and keep it under the mattress. Mummy writes things down too. The Man brings us paper, pencils, exercise books, and colouring books for me, but he doesn't speak much. Mummy tells me to keep out of his way, so I run to the toilet when he comes. Sometimes he finds me and smiles, and says that I'm getting a big girl. I don't like him. He's nearly as tall as the ceiling and he has hair all over his face. Mummy told me his name is Edwin, but I don't like him so I call him *The Man.*

Our house is small and dark. There's a light bulb hanging from the ceiling that stays on all the time, even when we go to sleep. It's too dark without the light on, and I get frightened. I get in bed with Mummy because there's nowhere else to sleep. When I lay in bed I can see all the rest of the house except the toilet and sink, which is around a little corner and out of the way. All the walls are greenish-grey, and Mummy says they're made out of concrete. When I touch them they're cold.

Mummy sticks my pictures on the walls with something called Blu-tack, and she says they brighten things up a bit. My best picture is the one of Prince, a ginger cat that some-times follows behind The Man when he brings our food. I'm allowed to stroke Prince until he goes back out, but then Mummy says I have to wash my hands before I eat anything.

Last week The Man brought me a reading book. I'd never had a reading book before. He said I had to look after it because he'd kept it safe for years since he was a little boy. It's got thick pages, large letters, and a sort of yellowy cardboard cover. I've started to read it. A lady called Enid Blyton wrote it, and it's called The Island of Adventure. It begins where a boy called Philip who loves animals is at some sort of summer school and is bored as he sits under a tree doing something called algebra (I asked Mummy what algebra is, and she said it's a different kind of maths). He hears a strange voice telling him to blow his nose and wipe his feet. It turns out the voice comes from a parrot sitting in a tree nearby, and he follows it as it flies off down the hillside back towards his school. That's the only bit I've read so far.

I asked Mummy what a parrot is, and why I can't sit under a tree. She told me a parrot is a colourful bird that flies around in hot countries, but that some people in this country keep them in cages as pets. I think that's cruel. If I had a parrot I'd let it fly about.

I had to ask her again why I can't sit under a tree. Mummy sighed and told me that trees grew outside, and we weren't allowed to go outside. When I asked her why, she said that The Man doesn't want us to.

It's boring in our house. I do maths with Mummy like Philip had to do at school. I know how to add up lots of numbers in my head and come up with the right answer, and Mummy says not many eight year olds can do that. She always asks me to spell words and read even longer words. She helps me with the ones I can't do, because she's a doctor and she's cleverer than me. When my felt tips run out I have to wait for The Man to bring more. There's no parrots flying around to look at, and I want to sit under a tree. One day I will get outside, but I'm not sure yet how I'll go about doing it.

The Man brought us some food a little while ago, but the sound of keys turning in the outer door and then the bolt shooting back tells me he is coming in again. I can hear him unlocking our door. Mummy jumps up and whispers to me to run and hide in the toilet, and not to come out until she tells me to.

I don't need to do a wee, so I sit on the plastic seat with my reading book. The light isn't very good in the toilet, and I have to hold the book close to my face. I hear the key opening the door to our house, and I hear footsteps on the bit of floor just inside the door that hasn't got any rough brown carpet on it.

I can't hear Mummy saying anything. I can hear the rustle of some sort of material, and after a while I can hear the noise that our bedsprings make when we wake up and turn over.

Nobody speaks, but I can hear The Man grunting away. Is he asleep? Mummy tells me never to come out of the toilet when he's here, but I can't see to read much and I want to find out why he's grunting. Perhaps if he's fallen asleep we can run to the door and get outside.

I put down my book and creep on tiptoe to the end of the wall and look around the corner. As soon as I do I want to cry, and wish I'd listened to Mummy.

Her eyes were closed. She was lying on her back and she looked sad. She had no clothes on and neither did The Man. I've never seen Mummy without any clothes on before. She has big boobs. I don't have any at all. The Man was fat and he was kneeling over her. Her hair had been taken out of its plait and was spread all over the pillow. I could see his bum moving backwards and forwards, but his face was pointing up towards the ceiling.

I run back to the safety of the toilet seat and cuddle my book close. My heart is beating fast, and it takes a long time to slow down. I try and work out why Mummy wants The Man to see her without any clothes on when she's always telling me that we have to cover up our private places.

The grunting stops and the bedsprings creak. I hear rustling again and footsteps going towards the door. The keys jangle, the door opens, but then closes quickly. I hear The Man locking it, shoving the bolt home, and walking to the outer door. The key turns in the lock, and then there's the sound of the other door being slammed shut and locked.

Mummy comes into the toilet. Holding onto my book I look down on the floor, because I don't want to see her without anything on. She lifts my chin up and smiles, but her eyes are sad. She has all her clothes back on. She says she needs a wee, and if I could sit on the bed then she will hear me read in a minute.

I skip to the bed, happy that The Man has gone. There is the sound of the sink filling up and splashing noises, and then Mummy is back with me.

I open the book. Philip runs back to school and meets Lucy-Ann. She has ginger hair like Prince. She's Jack's sister and has come to the school just to be with Jack in the summer holidays. I wish I had a brother or sister or a parrot. Jack loves birds and doesn't want to be at the school. He owns the parrot, whose name is Kiki. She's tame and sits on his shoulder. Jack is about fourteen, which is really old. He is older than me and Philip and Lucy-Ann. Philip has a sister called Dinah who is twelve and lives with their Aunt Polly at a big house near the sea called Craggy-Tops. I ask Mummy where the sea is, and she says there's lots and lots of salty water that's all around the British Isles where we live, and that water is the sea.

I want to see the sea, see the sea, and see the sea again. Mummy says I'm a very clever girl. I could even read the word 'ornithologist' in the book, but I don't know what it means. Because Mummy is a doctor she knows what everything means. She tells me it's somebody that likes and studies birds, and knows a lot about them. I've never seen a real bird. Jack wants to be an ornithologist when he grows up. I think I'll be one too and then I can have a parrot.

I draw a picture of the sea. Mummy says it's big and deep and cold, and has different names according to which country it surrounds. Between France and us is the English Channel. People swim the English Channel and it's about 21 miles and it takes them all day. I can't swim. Mummy washes my hair in the sink, but it's not big enough to swim in.

Jack and Lucy-Ann's parents were killed in a plane crash and they live with a horrible uncle. Philip and his sister Dinah have a mummy, but she has to work and so they live with their Uncle Jocelyn and Aunt Polly and a servant called Joe in a big half-ruined house with lots of rooms set halfway up a cliff. I live in a house that's got only one room, but like me they've only got a mummy.

I ask Mummy who my daddy is. Is it The Man? Mum-my smiles and shakes her head. She says The Man thinks he's my daddy, but he's not. She says we must never let The Man know that he isn't my daddy. She tells me that my real daddy is kind and loving and is a doctor that looks after children. The word begins with a 'p', but I can't remember how to spell it or say it. Mummy writes it down for me and gets me to read the word *paediatrician*. I can almost do it, but it's a hard word.

I have a daddy! I ask Mummy where he is, but she says she doesn't know. She tells me she met him when she was at medical school, studying to be a doctor. She smiles when she talks about him, and says he was already a doctor, but doing more studying to be children's doctor. She says he loved her and she loved him. They worked at the same hospital and were going to get married, but that was many years ago. She says his name is Liam Darrah.

How did they get me? I ask Mummy the question that has been bothering me for some time. She says they made me out of love, and that Daddy planted a seed inside her that grew into me. I try and imagine a seed growing into a tree, but instead it's inside Mummy and it grows into me. Instead of branches and leaves I have arms, hands and hair. If I lay on a branch my hair would hang down and parrots could climb up.

I'm hungry. I ask Mummy when The Man will be bringing us some food, but she says we have to wait. I fill our cups up with cold water from the sink, but it doesn't take away the hunger. He usually brings us food when we've been asleep for a long time, and then again twice more before we have go to sleep again. I don't want to read because my stomach's growling. Yesterday he brought us fish and chips because he said it was Friday. How does he know? Mummy says you can tell what day it is when you're outside because there are calendars and watches and newspapers, and it's bright during the day and dark at night. It's not bright in our house or dark either. It only gets dark if the light bulb wears out, and then I have to cuddle Mummy until The Man comes again and puts another one in.

When I hear the keys jangling and the bolt being pulled across and footsteps then I know The Man will bring us food. He always seems to bring something to eat when we're hungry. Sometimes I can smell the food before he unlocks the door if it's hot, but sometimes he brings sandwiches that don't smell of anything. That usually means it's going to be cheese or ham. I hate cheese. It's rubbery and floppy when you pick it out of the bread and hold it between your fingers. Mummy tells me off if I don't eat everything, but sometimes I can manage to put the cheese up my sleeve and flush it down the toilet later on, although once it wouldn't flush and kept coming back in the toilet bowl.

When we get hungry Mummy plaits my hair and ties it up and I plait hers, because she knows The Man will come soon. She says she doesn't want The Man to see our hair all loose and hanging down, but I don't know why. Today he brings us chicken pie, mash and peas. He says hello to me but I don't want to answer. Mummy says thank you but doesn't look up at him. He puts the plates of food down and picks up the dirty ones from breakfast, and then he goes away and locks the door.

We eat without saying anything. When I'm full and can't eat any more pie I push the plate away and open my reading book again.

Jack and Lucy-Ann's uncle has broken his leg and doesn't want them home for the rest of the school holidays, so he sends money to Jack's school to pay for them to stay there until their new school term begins. They pretend they're going to see Philip off on the train when he goes home, and at the last minute they jump on board the train and go with him to Craggy-Tops by the sea. Joe the servant picks them up at the station in his car. The school sends the money on to Craggy-Tops, and they live with Philip and Dinah's Aunt Polly and Uncle Jocelyn instead for the holidays. Jack is dying to see the seabirds, and Lucy-Ann just wants to be with Jack.

I ask Mummy what trains and cars are. She says they get people from one place to another faster than if they had to walk. I'd like to see a train and a car.

I want to go to Craggy-Tops with Philip, Jack, Lucy-Ann and Kiki the parrot. I don't want to stay in my boring house any more. I want to see my daddy who looks after children. I want him to look after *me*. Mummy always says I want too much, and that want doesn't get.

CHAPTER 4 – AMY

WHEN I GET too tired to read any more Mummy tells me it's time to clean my teeth and have a wash at the sink. The Man gives us toothpaste, soap, and clean flannels and towels. My towel is white with a green edging all the way around it. Mummy says she misses having a bath every day. I've never had a bath, but she says there's lots of water in it like the sea so I wouldn't like to have one in case I drown.

I get into bed and in my head I can hear the sea splashing all up the windows of Craggy-Tops. There's a picture of it in the book. Aunt Polly lets the boys sleep on a mattress in the tower room, and Jack looks out of the window over to the Isle of Gloom and sees all the birds flying around outside.

I look around and I can't see any windows. When I ask Mummy why we don't have any windows she says that the house wasn't built with any. I really want to see what's outside, but Mummy says Edwin wouldn't like us to go out, and it would make him really angry if we tried to leave the house.

I lie on my back in the bed and look up at the light bulb. It flickers a little bit and I'm frightened in case it goes out.

Mummy strokes my hair and says she will always be there and that I'll never be alone. I close my eyes and pretend I'm in the tower room at Craggy-Tops, looking over the sea towards the Isle of Gloom. Joe the servant told the children that nas-ty things happen on the island and that they mustn't go there.

They're not allowed to go to the island, and I'm not allowed to go outside.

Suddenly I'm awake and I sit up and panic because I can't see anything. I need a wee and I'm blind. Mummy wakes up next to me in bed, hears me crying, and puts her arms around me. She says that the light bulb has gone out and that Edwin needs to bring another one. I tell her I need a wee badly and she takes my hand and very slowly we climb out of bed and stand up.

I can't see where to go. Mummy says to hold her hand because she knows where the toilet is. I shake with fear. We walk very slowly in the dark and Mummy finds it. I feel the cold seat and lift up my nightie with one hand and clutch Mummy's hand with the other. It's hard to wipe myself afterwards, but I manage it.

As we creep along back to bed I wonder where the toilet is at Craggy-Tops. Are the corridors dark at night with no electricity? Does Jack have to wake up Philip and ask him where it is? Does he have to take an oil lamp with him to the toilet? Does Lucy-Ann know where the toilet is? What if there isn't a toilet? How did they flush the toilet when the water had to be drawn up from a well in the yard?

I cuddle Mummy and I fall asleep again. When we wake up it's not worth getting out of bed because we can't see anything. I reach under the bed and grab my book. We have to wait for The Man. I listen for the bolt being pulled back on the other door, and his keys in the door to our house. When he comes in Mummy asks him for another light bulb and he goes out and locks the door again. We wait for him to come back and I clutch my reading book to my chest in the dark, feeling its thick pages. It's nice to hold the book, even though I can't read it.

The Man comes back with a torch and some food and changes the light bulb. Mummy asks if we can keep the torch. The Man smiles at me when the light comes on, but I look away. I feel The Man's eyes staring at me, and he says that if I smile at him I would be able to keep the torch.

I don't know what to do. I look at Mummy but she has a smile that's fixed on her face. I want to keep the torch in case the light bulb breaks again, so I clutch my book and smile at The Man, and he reaches out and gives me the torch. Mummy asks have I forgotten my manners, so I thank him and look down at the torch, which is still warm from where he'd been holding it.

The Man goes away and locks the door. We eat our breakfast without really saying much. I'm worried in case Mummy is angry because I smiled at The Man, but when I ask her she says that I did the right thing. We have a torch to use now if the light bulb goes out again.

The Man pulls the bolt back on the door again soon after we've eaten. Mummy tells me to go and sit on the toilet, and I grab my book and run when I hear his keys jangling outside.

I feel safe on the toilet with my book, even though there isn't a door, because he doesn't usually try and find me.

This time I don't want to look around the corner. I can't hear anything, just the rustling of material, grunting, and the noise of the bedsprings. When I hear his footsteps going towards the door I hear Mummy asking him for towels and nappy bags because she says her period is due. The Man doesn't say anything.

What's a nappy bag? When she comes to find me I hold up our towels and tell her The Man brought us some. She shakes her head and tells me that she wants a different kind of towel, one that I'll have to use when I'm a bit older. She says all girls have to use them once they get to about twelve or thirteen years of age. I ask her if I can see one, and she says I'll have to wait until Edwin brings them and then she'll show one to me.

The next day Mummy says she has a tummy ache. She lies on the bed and clutches at her stomach. I ask her if she's eaten something nasty, but she shakes her head and says she has a period. I don't know what she means, so she explains about girls' bodies making eggs that either turn into babies or they don't. If they don't, then the body gets rid of the unwanted egg. It comes out when a girl does a wee, and there's a lot of blood but it's normal. Sometimes there would be a lot of pain and other times there wouldn't be, but all girls keep getting rid of eggs from about the age of twelve until they grow really old at about 50.

That's a lot to think about. I'm about 8 or 9, but I don't think I'm going to get any periods. I don't really want them because they don't sound very nice, and I'm sure that Dinah and Lucy-Ann don't have periods because they never talk about them, or towels or eggs. Mummy took a towel out of the packet that The Man brought and showed me. It's long and thick, and you have to put it between your legs and then put your knickers on. Ugh, it's horrible.

Mummy has to keep running to the toilet when she has a period. I see that she puts the towels she has used into the nappy bags and puts them in the rubbish bin. She ties the handles of the bags really tightly together. After a few days she smiles again and says her tummy ache has gone, and then I'm happy because I have my normal mummy back again.

When Mummy has a tummy ache she doesn't do any exercises, and The Man doesn't come down and creak the bedsprings. When her period goes she says I have to keep using all my muscles, and she shows me how to do sit-ups and handstands and shoulder stands. We have to jog on the spot for ages and it's boring. I can hear my heart beating fast and she says that's good, but I say it's bad because I'd rather sit down with my reading book or add up lots of numbers in my head. My head is full of numbers and words that I have to write down before I forget them all.

I know The Man will soon be coming back again and I'll have to sit on the toilet and try to read my book. I don't know why I have to sit on the toilet when the bedsprings are creaking, but I think next time I'm going to have another look. I hear him pulling back the bolt on the door outside.

Jack wanted to have a closer look at The Isle of Gloom, even though Joe had told him that bad things went on there. He knew the seabirds would be tame because nobody lived there now and the birds were not used to seeing people. He wanted to go to the island and see if there were any rare birds and take photos, but Joe wouldn't lend out his boat.

I wonder if it would be fun to go on a boat? I wouldn't want to go to the Isle of Gloom though, because it sounds too scary. One day I'll get Mummy and Daddy to take me on a boat ride.

The book is really exciting and even though The Man came in and started to creak the bedsprings I didn't care, and I couldn't wait to see what was on the next page. I took the torch into the toilet and shone it on the pages. The boys had fallen through a hole in the floor of a cave into a secret tunnel, and had lit a candle because like me they couldn't see anything. Kiki didn't like the dark. My torch picked out the words as they crept along the tunnel that ended at a wall and a trapdoor above their heads. Philip climbed up on Jack and got through the trapdoor, and then he hauled Jack up. Then Philip recognised they were in one of the cellars at Craggy-Tops; one he hadn't been in before. They can't get out because the door is locked, and then they have to hide because they hear Joe's footsteps coming towards the cellar door and opening it.

Mummy comes into the toilet looking sad and says that she needs a wee. That was annoying because I was in Craggy-Tops' cellar with my torch. Mummy takes the torch away and says it's time for my lessons and that we have to save the battery in case the light bulb goes out. I go and sit on the bed and pretend I'm in the same cellar as Philip and Jack, and that The Man's footsteps are Joe's. He's just as nasty as Joe anyway, so I'm going to call him Joe now. I have a look around my house, but Joe's gone.

CHAPTER 5 - AMY

MUMMY'S HAD A wash and she's smiling again. I plait her hair because Joe, The Man, had undone it. I think I'd like to do algebra like Philip, so I ask Mummy if she knows how to do it. She says yes and I learn about x being the variable and then I have to find out what x is in a sum. Sometimes I can do it, and sometimes Mummy makes the sum too hard, but then she shows me how to find the right answer.

I get bored with algebra, so Mummy teaches me about my body. I learn the names of bones and muscles, and how the muscles and ligaments will move my bones to where they want to go. I ask if my quad muscles can move my femurs so that they are outside the house, but Mummy says Edwin has to unlock the door first and then leave it unlocked, because femurs, tibias and fibulas can't walk through closed doors.

I try and think of my heart pumping all the blood around my body. I can feel it sometimes if I jump up and down, but I can't see it. It pumps away even before we are born. Mummy says that if you listen with a special instrument you can hear a baby's heart beating while it's still inside its mother's womb.

How does the baby get out from the womb? Does it climb out? Does all the climbing out make its heart beat faster and faster? I ask Mummy if I climbed out of her womb. She says that it took many hours for me to come out, and at the end she pushed me out onto the bed we're sitting on with her pelvic floor muscles. I didn't feel her pushing me though, so I must have been asleep. I asked her if anybody caught me as she pushed me out, but she said that she pushed me out on her own and caught me herself.

She says that sometimes babies can't be pushed out and that the mother has to go to hospital for the baby to be cut out by a doctor. I want to know where the babies are pushed out from, and Mummy says they come out from the hole where you do a wee, which can stretch to be as big as a baby's head.

I don't understand hours because there are no clocks in our house. Mummy draws clocks sometimes and says that they usually have three hands that move around, but I've never seen one. Do the hands move slowly? I want to see one, but all I get told is that want doesn't always get.

When is it daytime? Mummy says it's when the sun shines brightly and it's light outside and you can see everything around you. At night it becomes dark and you have to turn the lights on to see. We don't have daytime in our house, so probably that's why we don't need a clock.

I need to find out what happened to Jack, Philip and Kiki.

Joe comes into the cellar where the boys are hiding, but Kiki makes a sound like Joe coughing, and Joe gets really frightened and runs, touching the boys by accident in the dark on the way out and getting even more scared, and then he gets told off by Aunt Polly in the kitchen. Jack and Philip laugh a lot to think Joe was frightened of them, and find he was so scared that he left his key in the cellar door. They take it and go through the door into the part of the cellar that Philip knows, to find boxes were in the way that had hidden the door, and Philip hadn't known the door was there. He felt excited about finding it.

How can I make Joe frightened of me? The light is always on in our house because it's never daytime, so he can always see me. If he can't see me he knows that I'll be sitting on the toilet.

Perhaps when I hear his footsteps I can run and turn off the light and then run out of the door when he opens it, but where can I turn off the light? I get up and walk around our house, looking for something to turn it off with. Mummy asks me what on earth am I doing, but I just say I'm going for a walk.

I can't find anything that turns off the light. I look up and there's a wire that goes from the light bulb up into the ceiling. I can't reach up to the ceiling and there are no trapdoors up above like Jack and Philip found. It's not fair; how is it that they can find a trapdoor and I can't?

There's nothing else to do except to carry on reading.
I'm going to have to think of another plan....

Jack and Philip creep up the cellar steps into the kitchen, but nobody's about so they go to the outer door and run down the cliff path again to the cave where Dinah and Lucy-Ann were still waiting for them to come out of the tunnel. Philip creeps into the cave and throws a starfish at Dinah and makes her jump.

Dinah hates her brother. I wish I had a brother or sister; I wouldn't hate them at all. Mummy says she doesn't want another baby, because I'm quite enough for her to look after, and anyway the house isn't big enough. I ask her if we can have a house as big as Craggy-Tops, but Mummy says no.

I hear the bolt sliding back and Joe's footsteps at the door. Mummy gives me *that* look so I slide off the bed, grab my book, and run to the toilet as keys jangle in the lock outside. We haven't long eaten, so I think Joe wants to take Mummy's hair out of its plait again and spread it on her pillow. Mummy stands up to wait for him.

I wish I could read in the toilet, but if I try to it hurts my eyes. I hold the book against me and listen, and wait for Joe to stop making the bedsprings creak. When the noise stops I hear him say that something has split, but that's all he says and there's no reply from Mummy. I hear a zip being done up and I clutch my book to me, hoping he'll go straight out.

He doesn't. He comes to the toilet, the place where I try and hide, and stands in front of me. I hate him. He fills the toilet with his great body and looks down on me. I pretend to like him and smile. I can see Mummy standing behind him with her hair all loose and hanging down, and I want him to go away. He asks me if I like the reading book, and I nod.

He says he wants me to call him Daddy. He says if I don't call him Daddy he'll take my reading book away. Behind him I can see Mummy nodding as though she wants me to say yes, but I remember her saying that my daddy is called Liam. She's nodding really hard and looks as though her head is going to fall off. I want to laugh at Mummy's head going up and down, but then look at Joe and the bubbling laughter inside dies away.

I can see that the only way to make him go away is to give him what he wants. I tell him I will call him Daddy, and Mummy's head stops nodding. He turns around to Mummy and takes some of her hair in his hands and strokes it, before unlocking the door and going back out.

Mummy says she needs a wee and that I was a very good girl, but I tell her how can I be good when I've told a lie? She smiles and says that sometimes in life you have to tell little white lies that aren't as bad as actual lies so that people don't get angry and hurt you. Thinking about what might happen if Daddy gets too angry, I see that Mummy is probably right and I'm glad I lied to him.

Daddy's gone and I can sit on the bed and read again. There's a wet patch on the duvet that smells funny, so I move away from it and sit on the other side.

CHAPTER 6 – AMY

JACK LIES IN the grass at the top of a cliff looking through binoculars at the Isle of Gloom. He sees somebody rowing near Craggy-Tops in a boat and thinks it must be Joe, but on his way back to the house he sees that Joe's boat is still there. He tells the others he's seen somebody with a boat, and Philip says they should try and find the owner of the boat and make friends.

That night they look out of the window of the tower room and see Joe sailing his boat towards the shore with some cargo on board. They creep down to the harbour where Joe's boat was heading and jump out at him, making him fall into the water in fright. He comes out of the water very angry and hits Jack, but Philip charges into Joe's middle and makes him gasp for breath. Then the boys run along the beach with Joe chasing after them and disappear down the secret tunnel in the cave, but they have to find their way back to the cellar in complete darkness. Joe doesn't know about the secret passage and waits outside the cave for them, but wonders if it was Jack and Philip on the beach when they appear at breakfast the next morning as if nothing had happened.

I was glad I didn't make Daddy angry. He might have hit me like Joe had hit Jack. Mummy never makes him angry either. I think I'll pretend I like Daddy and smile and smile, and then he might give me what I want. I want some new clothes because the ones I've got are too small; the sleeves are halfway up my arms, and my trouser legs are way above my ankles now and the waist is too tight. Mummy already asked him for clothes, but he never brought any. She always tells me that want doesn't get.

I smile at Daddy when he brings our dinner and I ask him for some bigger clothes. Mummy looks surprised and says I should mind my manners and say please. I smile again and say please, and then look down at my book. Daddy smiles back at me and says he will bring some clothes and some more pencils and colouring books. I make sure I say thank you to Daddy and smile again. He goes away I feel warm inside, because not only can I keep my reading book, I'm now going to get some new clothes and pencils and colouring books as well.

Mummy doesn't really want me to talk to Daddy, but I don't see why I can't. He's horrible, but he seems to like me more now I smile at him.

When we wake up Daddy brings our breakfast and our lunchtime sandwiches, and he also brings a larger pair of black trousers, a blue and white dress, two bigger jumpers (one red and one green), and white socks and knickers the next size up for me. I've never seen so many clothes and I smile and smile as though my life depended on it. From the pockets of his overalls Daddy brings me pencils, paper, colouring books, and a big bar of chocolate. My mouth changes into an 'o' shape, and I remember to call him Daddy and say thank you. It's hard to talk when I have to smile so much. He says he is going to work, but he will bring dinner later on. He goes out and turns the key in the lock, and I hear the bolt sliding across on the outer door.

I look at Mummy and she looks at me, and we both burst out laughing. She says she will have to try smiling at him as well. I try on the jumpers and they fit. The dress is a bit big, but Mummy says I'll grow into it. The trousers are a little bit too long, so I turn them up at the bottom.

I do some colouring with my new pencils after breakfast, and then it's time for me to jog on the spot. The trouser bottoms start coming down again when I jog, and Mummy says she wishes she had a needle and thread. I say that I'll smile at Daddy and ask, but she shakes her head and says he'd never give us any needles.

Daddy brought us ham and tomato sandwiches for lunch and some fruitcake. There are bits of seeds inside the tomatoes that fall out of the bread onto my new jumper. I run to the sink and wipe them off, and then pick up my reading book.

The children are swimming in the sea. Philip swam out to some rocks and climbed on them to rest, and saw the boat tethered on the other side of the rocks that Jack had seen a few days before. They go exploring and find a hut built into a cliff, and a man comes out when he hears the children. He says his name is Bill Smugs and that he's a bird watcher. The children make friends with him and he takes them out in his boat for trips and for a ride into town in his car, where they buy torches so that they don't have to use candles in their bedrooms and in the secret tunnel. They see Joe in town and he has no idea how they could have travelled there.

Joe watches them as they go into a posh hotel to meet Bill for lunch. He sits outside and waits for them to come out, but the children and Bill go out the back way and Joe is angry when he returns to Craggy Tops and sees the children there.

I wonder if Daddy would be angry if I could find a back way out of my house and meet my real daddy for lunch in the same posh hotel? How can I escape? I look at the greeny-grey walls with my pictures stuck on them, but can't see any other way to get out except through the door that Daddy al-ways keeps locked. There's no secret tunnel either, because I've already checked. How come that Jack and Philip could find one but I can't?

Perhaps there's a door hidden under one of my pictures? I pull some of the Blu-tack away on one corner of the picture of Prince while Mummy is in the toilet, but there's only more wall behind it.

I ask why the door is always locked. Mummy looks sad when she says that Daddy wants to keep us inside the house and doesn't want us to get out. I feel scared that I might never get outside to see the sea and caves and hotels and par-rots until I'm grown up. Mummy cuddles me and says that my real daddy will be searching for us, and that we must be brave and not complain because we must not make Daddy cross.

Mummy says it's time for singing. I like singing; it makes me feel happy inside. She teaches me a new song by somebody called Rolling Stones. It's called 'You Can't Always Get What You Want.' My voice sounds like Mummy's when I sing, and as I learn the words I find out that if I try sometimes, I might find I get what I need.

I'm going to try and get what I want. I really want to get out of my house, so I have to try and please Daddy so that I can get what I need.

CHAPTER 7 - AMY

JOE STARTS FOLLOWING the children everywhere. He knows they've found a way to get into town and he wants to find out who is giving them a lift, because there's no other way to get into town except by car. The children outwit him and go into the cave and down the secret tunnel that leads back to Craggy-Tops' cellars. Joe waits outside the cave for them to return, but instead they escape and go to find Bill Smugs, who agrees to take them sailing out near the Isle of Gloom.

Daddy starts appearing more and more as Mummy and I keep on smiling at him, but I don't know what to do to out-wit him. I feel as though he's following me with his eyes, just like Joe was following the children. The only way I can escape from him looking at me is to sit on the toilet with my book, but if he doesn't want to creak the bedsprings with Mummy he tells me to come back into the house because he says we're getting to be a proper little family now.

I look at Daddy and smile as he brings me chocolates, felt tip pens, jigsaw puzzles and drawing paper. He brings us a little table and three chairs that only just fits in our house, and now I don't have to sit on the bed and eat and it's easier to do my lessons at the table. Sometimes when he brings us food he sits there with us and eats his dinner at the same time. I don't like him sitting with us, but we mustn't make him cross and so we smile and pretend we're happy. He looks at me and tells Mummy that he has a beautiful daugh-ter, that I'm his princess, and that no other man must ever get to look at me or at her. I want to tell him he's not my real father, but then I remember that Mummy says he must never know.

Mummy smiles all the time Daddy is there, but now looks sad most of the time when he's not. I hear her crying sometimes when she thinks I'm asleep.

The best time is when we know Daddy has to go to work and we know he won't be visiting us. He leaves us our lunch and says he will be back at dinnertime, but now Mummy doesn't even look happy when he's gone for a while. She doesn't even want to eat much either, and leaves some of her sand-wiches on the plate. She says she feels sick, and sometimes she retches down the toilet and is sick. I worry there's some-thing wrong with her and that she's going to die.

Mummy says she is not ill, but she knows she is going to have another baby and she cries because she doesn't want it. I ask her how she knows, and she says her periods have stopped, her boobs are sore, and her tummy already feels tighter and rounder. I ask her how she got the baby, and she tells me that Edwin put it in there.

I'm going to have a brother or sister! If it's a boy I'll have a brother the same as Dinah or Lucy-Ann now! I dance around the house with happiness, but Mummy says the baby will be my stepsister or stepbrother and not a real one, and this is because I have a different daddy.

I don't care. I'll be able to help Mummy wash the baby in the sink, and dry it with my towel with green edges on, and feed it with all the cheese sandwiches I don't like. This is the best thing that has happened since Daddy brought me some new clothes. I'm too excited to read any more of my book and can't wait to tell Daddy the news when he comes home from work, but Mummy tells me not to say anything, and that she will tell him all in good time.

I ask Mummy how long I have to wait before the baby is born. She says it will take 9 months for the baby to grow in her tummy, but she thinks it has already been growing for about 2 months. She says it will be many days before the baby gets here, but I have already worked out that I only have to wait 7 more months though.

What is a month? I don't really understand days and weeks and months, but Mummy repeats that because our house has no windows we then don't see any daylight, and so cannot see the days going by. She tells me that a month is about 30 days, but as I've never even seen a day I don't know what she's talking about. If it's only 7 months, then that can't be too long as I can count up to 7 on my fingers. She explains that one day is 24 hours, but there are no clocks in our house and I can't think of what an hour looks like.

Daddy brings us fish and fried potatoes and peas. I'm bursting to tell him about the baby, but Mummy shoots me a look with her eyes and I know I must smile and keep quiet and to remember that it's a secret. Daddy eats with us at the table, but Mummy can't eat much again. She tells Daddy she has a tummy upset, and he takes her plate of food away and locks the door.

If the baby is a girl I asked Mummy if we can call her Lucy-Ann, and Mummy said yes because it's a very nice name. If it's a boy I ask if we can call him Jocelyn the same as Philip's uncle, but Mummy says no son of hers is ever go-ing to be called Jocelyn.

I want the baby to hurry up and get here. After a while Mummy stops feeling sick and starts wanting to eat food again. I can see her tummy is a bit bigger, and she says she will have to tell Daddy soon. I ask her why she hasn't told him sooner, and she says that sometimes the eggs that turn into babies come out too early and are flushed away down the toilet. I'm pleased that Lucy-Ann is still in Mummy's tummy though, but she says it's no world to bring a baby into.

Daddy comes home from work and brings roast beef, roast potatoes, broccoli and carrots and gravy. It's nice. I eat and look at Mummy, waiting for her to say something. Daddy looks at me and I smile at him. He smiles back.

Mummy tells Daddy she's going to have another baby. He stops eating and stares at her and asks if she's certain. She says yes. She says the room won't be big enough for three people, and Daddy says it will have to be because that's all there is. He doesn't want any more dinner and goes away, leaving us to eat in peace. He doesn't come back to take away the plates, and we spend the rest of the time before bed singing with joy because he's gone.

I smile my brightly when he opens the door and wakes us up with our breakfast, and he tells Mummy it took him a bit of time to get used to the idea of being a father again. He eats breakfast with us and then tells me to go and sit on the toilet with my book because he wants to talk to Mummy. I clutch my book and try to read as I hear the bedsprings creak and hear him telling Mummy in a low voice how good it feels without a rubber. Mummy tells him he is harming the baby, but he doesn't answer.

The children are all in the boat with Bill Smugs and he teaches them how to sail. As they circle around the Isle of Gloom Jack thinks he sees a rare bird called a Great Auk, but Bill tells him it isn't. He finds an old map of the Isle of Gloom in Uncle Jocelyn's study, and he sees a possible entrance to the island through a break in the rocks.

That night Jack looks out from the window in the tower room and sees a light coming from the island going on and off, and another light sending some sort of signal from the top of the cliff near Craggy-Tops. He wants to find out what's going on, so he gets dressed and creeps out.

I hear zips being done up and I haul myself back from the tower room at Craggy-Tops. I'm sitting on the toilet with my book and Daddy's come to find me. He asks if I'm looking forward to seeing the new baby, and I nod and smile. He says our family is growing and it makes him happy.

He goes out and locks the door, and Mummy comes in for a wee. I ask her what a rubber is, and she says it's used for rubbing out mistakes if you've written something down wrong with a pencil. I didn't know Daddy had written anything down wrong, but why did he say it felt good if he didn't have a rubber to rub it out with then?

I go back to Craggy-Tops while Mummy is in the toilet. Jack runs along the cliff top towards the light, but then Joe grabs him and asks him what he's up to. Kiki bites Joe's ear and Jack manages to escape back up to the tower room. He wakes up Philip and tells him what has happened, and says that he wants to use Joe's boat to go over to the Isle of Gloom.

If I had a parrot I could get it to bite Daddy's ear, then Mummy and I could escape through the door to the outside. We would have to run really fast though, so that Daddy couldn't catch us. We could then find a boat and sail to another island.

The boys wait until Joe has to take the car into town to get some shopping, and then they take his boat. They find the gap in the rocks that was on the map, and sail across to the Isle of Gloom and haul the boat up on the beach. They don't find a Great Auk, but before they return to the boat they do find lots of deep holes going down into the earth, one with quite a good ladder, and also old tins of food near-by.

I get to wondering if our house has a cellar or a hole in the ground that Mummy and I could climb down and escape. I look at the floor but it's made of the same grey-green stuff as the walls, and it's as solid as solid can be. I stamp my feet on it, but it doesn't move. I wonder if Jack and Philip would have managed to find a way out of our house? They seem so real that I feel I could reach out and touch them in the book. I know they would help if they could only find us. If they could manage to get hold of Joe's boat again they would just have to sail around our island and look out for a house without any windows.

Mummy says if I put my hand on her tummy I can feel the baby move. I ask if it is Lucy-Ann or Jocelyn in there but she says she doesn't know, and that no son of hers is ever going to be called Jocelyn anyway.

One day Daddy brings larger clothes for Mummy, because her tummy is getting really big. He doesn't seem to want to creak the bedsprings any more, and instead he eats his dinners with us at the table and strokes her belly sometimes. She always closes her eyes when he does that, and I can see that she doesn't really like him doing it. He's also started stroking my hair and wanting me to sit on his lap. He tells me I'm his princess again. I hate him and he smells of really strong scent. Mummy says he uses a lot of aftershave and that's why he smells funny. She says I mustn't make him cross so I have to pretend I like sitting on his legs.

Lucy-Ann doesn't have to sit on Bill Smugs' lap, so why must I sit on Daddy's? I don't want to be his princess; it's horrible. He puts his arms around me and says what a beautiful girl I am. He says he would never let anybody hurt me or make me cry. I can usually get away though by saying I have to go to the toilet. If I try and stay in there as long as possible, he gets fed up and goes back to his own house and locks the door.

While the boys were gone Lucy-Ann and Dinah locked Joe in the secret room in the cellar so he couldn't see his boat was missing. Philip crept down to the cellar and quietly undid the lock while Joe was coughing, then ran upstairs again. All four children pretended they had just come in from a walk when Joe appeared and accused them of locking him in, but Aunt Polly told him not to be so silly.

Dinah took her Uncle Jocelyn something to eat and stole his map of the Isle of Gloom that showed all the holes leading down to the old copper mines, and on the back was a map of all the underground tunnels on the island that miners worked in to dig out the copper. She thought people might be still working in the mines because the boys had found tins of food. The children were determined to sail over to the island again and explore the mines.

I wish I could steal Daddy's keys, lock him in our house, and then run away with Mummy.

Daddy sometimes leaves us tins of food if he's going to be at work for a long time. He leaves Mummy a tin opener and spoons, but we're never allowed knives or forks. I've never seen a knife, but Mummy says it's sharp and you can cut yourself with it. She always says she hates eating with a spoon.

I keep waiting for the baby to come, but Mummy says it will be a few more months. She tries again to explain about minutes, hours, days, weeks and months, but I can't understand it all very much. All I know is that I want to see my little baby stepsister Lucy-Ann. I don't really want a stepbrother now, just in case he looks too much like Daddy.

CHAPTER 8 - BETH

IF ONLY EDWIN hadn't given Amy that book. I had managed to keep her virtually unaware of the seriousness of our situation, but now the book has brought the outside in, and Amy is restless. I see her walking around the room looking for a way out, but there is none. I know, because I have tried many, many times to find an escape route. She is becoming older and more aware, and it is becoming harder and harder to keep up the pretence.

I can see she that feels the same distaste for Edwin as I do. I dread what will happen when she turns into a woman. She will be stunning. I see Edwin beginning to take more notice of her now, but I'm not sure if that's because he thinks she is his daughter and is proud of her, or because he is starting to find her sexually attractive. Soon maybe I will not be enough for him. I pray to God to get us out of here before her breasts grow and she is able to bear children. I wonder if God is listening to my prayers, and lately I wonder if he really exists at all. What have I done to displease Him so much?

I feel the baby moving around inside me. I pray to anybody who is listening that it will be a boy. A boy will not interest Edwin sexually, and will grow the strong muscles I do not possess that could one day overpower our captor. With a boy we have a good chance of escaping in maybe 15 or 16 years time, as Edwin grows older and weaker. Now he is powerfully strong; I feel his strength as he lies on top of me. He could kill me with one of his huge hands, and there is no point in trying to resist. I struggled to get away the first time, and I was beaten so badly I nearly lost Amy. I have learned my lesson. I endure and stay silent. It's the best way.

I see Liam's face every day when I look at his daughter. It's there in her eyes and in the special way she smiles, and she has his sunny temperament.

Liam; I remember his soft Canadian accent and his habit of turning any statement into a question. It's getting harder to remember his actual features, but Amy will always be here to remind me. He was much taller than Edwin; about 6 feet 2inches. He used to let me clipper his floppy fair hair close to his head in the summer, and he cared not a jot about his appearance. Amy has his mathematical, logical brain.

Edwin only sees her long silky blonde hair, but Amy has her father's brain underneath that could maybe outwit him one day in the not-too-distant future. She could be virtually anything she wanted to be, but alas for our present predicament, not a prize-fighter. I imagine she is streets ahead of any state school pupil of the same age. She knows the names of all the bones and muscles in the body. She's accomplished at long division and long multiplication and algebra, she reads quickly and with understanding, and she is a pleasure to teach. I fill my days with teaching Amy or writing in this diary, and there is nothing else I can do to pass the time.

Our prison must only be about 10ft by 8ft, not including the toilet. How on earth can three people live in it for the rest of their days without going insane? Even now I wonder if I am losing my mind. I hear myself snap at Amy sometimes if she asks the same question more than once, but I immediately feel remorse.

I crave sunlight and fresh air. I want to know what the date and the time is. I want to read a newspaper. I don't know which season it is, how old I am, or on which date Amy was born. I know it must have been sometime in late December 1987, but when I delivered her myself on our bed I had lost track of the days. The worst thing is having no idea of time; the only way I can measure it of course is by Edwin's presentation of meals. I know it is a Sunday lunchtime when he brings us a roast dinner, but on other days we have to eat sandwiches while he is at work so we eat when we're hungry. The days are endless.

I lumber about the confines of my prison, my mood lowering with every passing day. My daughter should not be subjected to the sight of a woman in labour at her age. There is nowhere else for the baby to be born except on the bed, where Amy herself once entered this cruel world.

For something to do I dredge up my midwifery training and teach Amy about the development of the foetus, and draw diagrams depicting how the baby changes in the womb with every passing month. Amy is fascinated, and says she wants to be a midwife when she grows up. I hate to crush her enthusiasm and youthful ambitions, but the only chance she may ever have to be a midwife is to help deliver her half-brother or sister. The thought that she and the new baby may have to spend their entire life imprisoned in this room scares me beyond words.

I spend some time informing Amy that when labour starts I am going to be in severe pain, but that she must not panic. I tell her I am not ill, and that the pain will disappear when the baby is born. She listens carefully.

The baby's head has not engaged and I must be near to full-term now. I seem to spend hours now on all fours with my head on the floor, just willing the baby to turn. Amy laughs as I rock and sway from side to side like a belly dancer, but I also know from my midwifery training all those years ago that the baby is in a transverse lie, the worst presentation of all.

My last plan of action is to use our torch to shine a light on my pubic bone. I tell Amy that she has to get used to seeing me without any knickers on, as this is what midwives have to do if she wants to learn how to help catch a baby when it's born. I lie like a beached whale on the bed and ask her to shine the torch and shout directly onto my pubis. I know we're wasting precious batteries in the faint hope that the baby will hear her voice and turn towards the light, but I'm gambling on anything now.

Amy is asleep when I awake, needing to use the toilet. My bladder is the size of a cherry these days. The show of blood-stained mucus confirms the beginning of labour. I try not to panic as I feel the baby's buttocks are still over to one side of my abdomen and its head is over on the other side. There is no room left to try and turn the baby. A shoulder presentation is any mother's worst nightmare. I need a caesarean section. The baby will not be born without one.

I dress in a bra, knickers, skirt and jumper, and lie back down on the bed and try to breathe deeply to slow down my pounding heart rate. I don't know what the time is or how long Amy will sleep for. I need Edwin to bring breakfast to let him know I need an ambulance.

I suddenly feel full of hope: an ambulance will take me to hospital, and I will be able to speak to the anaesthetist before they put me under. Better still I can write a note on Amy's drawing paper with her felt tips. I slide out of bed again as gently as I can, and as I feel the first contraction I write in big letters that I have been held against my will for about 8 or 9 years by the man that has brought me into hospital. I do not remember his surname or know his address, but I know his name is Edwin, and he is also keeping my daughter there as a prisoner. I write down my parents' names and their last known address, and I fold up the paper and pop it into my bra for safekeeping.

Amy stirs eventually as the contractions are gripping me about every ten minutes. I take off my knickers but keep my skirt on. There is a rush of blooded water onto the bed-clothes, and I can feel the umbilical cord presenting in the birth canal. I explain to her that she cannot help the baby to be born because I need to go to hospital, and that the baby will not be born unless I can have an operation. She holds her reading book with one hand for comfort, and hammers on the door in panic with the other hand shouting for Edwin.

Whether he heard her or whether it was time for him to bring us breakfast I do not know, but he arrived and nearly dropped the tray of food as he saw the bedclothes and my face. I explain the transverse lie which needs a caesarean section, and that both myself and the baby are at risk. I plead with him to call an ambulance.

Edwin tries to keep the panic from his voice, and says that as I'm a doctor and I delivered Amy, then I can deliver the baby myself. I explain that this baby is presenting shoulder first and not head first like Amy did, and that if he wants both of us to live then he needs to get me to hospital as quickly as possible.

Edwin says no ambulances. Amy hugs her book looking distraught, and pleads with him to take me to hospital in his car. He appears stunned, and stands there not knowing what to do. I am gripped by a fierce contraction as my body tries in vain to expel the baby. The pain doubles me up on the bed and Amy screams in panic.

Amy's screaming seems to jolt Edwin out of his stupor. He runs out and locks the door, but then comes back in with a carrier bag of food and says it's for Amy. Prince follows him. He tells her to be a good girl and look after Prince, and that he will be back after the baby has been born. I cry and plead with him to take Amy with us, but he insists that she must stay. He says to her that he was often left on his own from the age of about four in a cupboard and survived, and that she must be a brave girl. He picks me up as though I was as light as a feather, and carries me through the door that has been closed to me for nine or so years. He locks up after us, and my heart goes out to my daughter, sobbing alone on the other side of the door. I can hear her little hands pound-ing on the woodwork as she calls out for me.

Edwin tells me to shut my eyes. He carries me up some stairs and opens another door. I peep through my closed eyelids and find we are in the kitchen of his house. I see a clock on the wall, which says 6.30. I assume it must be early morning instead of night-time, as Amy had not long been awake and no daylight is coming through the drawn curtains. He carries on up the hallway, opens the front door and goes through a sort of half porch, and I am outside for the first time in nearly a decade.

I feel cold, cold air. I hear the crunch of his footsteps on snow. He tells me to keep my eyes closed. Another contraction takes my breath away. He opens the car door with one hand and helps me into the front seat. I try and slouch so as not to compress the umbilical cord, which is partly hanging out of the birth canal. I ask him to lay the seat down, and he complies. The seat cover feels furry, and I pull at it until some of the fur comes off in my hands. I hold on to the fur. He tells me that if I open my eyes he will kill Amy.

He starts the car and we move off. I open my eyes just the tiniest amount and can see we are in a street with other houses. Nobody is about. I'm laid too far down and it's too dark to see any sign that might give me the name of the street. I feel him looking at me as he drives, and realise I must be very careful not to put Amy at any risk.

I see road signs flashing by, and caught a glimpse of an arrow pointing straight ahead to Croydon. I remember that Croydon is a large outer London suburb on the border with Surrey.

I get a flashback to the evening of 20th May 1987; the last time I saw his car. I was 27, and remembered how happy I had been when starting out on that short walk back to the accommodation unit. If only I had known what was going to happen when I leaned inside the passenger window to speak to him. I recall how creepy he seemed when he told me I had beautiful hair as I treated him on the triage trolley. I must have inhaled something like chloroform or ketamine that night, but I suppose I'll never really know what happened. I was on cloud nine as I knew I was pregnant, but I never had the chance to tell Liam, and to this day he has no idea he has a daughter.

We arrive at the hospital and he tells me not to say a word or Amy will die. He says he will speak for me, and that he will not leave my side for even a minute. In-between contractions I can still feel the piece of paper in my bra, and I hope and pray I can get it to one of the nurses without him noticing.

CHAPTER 9 - BETH

HE PARKS THE car and carries me into Accident & Emergency. He's sweating despite the cold morning, and drips of perspiration drop down his face. I'm in terrible pain but think of Amy locked in the room and I say nothing. I hold on tightly to the piece of fur from the seat cover. I notice a sign giving information in the waiting area. It says that the date is Friday January 5th 1996. I realise I am nearly 36 years old and heading towards middle age. The clerk on reception wants to take my name, address, and date of birth, but Edwin gives false details and gives an address in Scotland that he probably made up on the spot. He reiterates to the clerk that we do not live in the area, but were visiting relatives when labour started.

I'm ushered straight in to a cubicle. The doctor pulls the curtains around me and asks Edwin to wait on the other side while he examines me. I can hear him breathing close by as I change into a gown, and I hold the precious piece of paper and the fur under my arm. The fur is of a nondescript greyish colour. The doctor examines me, takes some observations, and says that I need an emergency caesarean to save the baby. I tell him I have not eaten or drunk anything for at least 6 hours, and he rings up to Theatre to inform them to prepare for me. Another contraction makes me want to retch. A porter arrives with a wheelchair to take me up to Theatre. Edwin follows close behind, but is barred from en-try at the doors to the operating suite.

I thought there was going to be a scuffle, but at the last minute Edwin gives in and says he will be waiting for me to come out, and to remember his promise. I shiver inside as I'm wheeled through the doors of the operating suite and into the anaesthetic room.

At last after nearly 10 years I am free of him. I bring out the piece of paper and the fur from under my arm. The paper is warm and folded up into a tiny square. I give it to the anaesthetist as another contraction makes me temporarily lose my grip on reality. I gasp and tell the anaesthetist that my name is Dr Elizabeth Nichols, and that I was kidnapped from the Rachelle hospital in Norfolk, on 20th May 1987 by the man waiting outside, whose name I only know as Edwin. I tell him my 9-year-old daughter Amy is still being held prisoner in Edwin's house, and that he has threatened to kill her if he finds out I have spoken to anybody. I tell him I do not know Edwin's address. I also give him the piece of fur from the car seat. The anaesthetist gives me a stunned sort of look and assures me that one of the team will contact the police, but in the interim time is of the essence and that he must anaesthetise me because the baby is in severe distress.

He places an oxygen mask over my face and I breathe in deeply to help the baby. I thank the life inside me for giving me the means to escape, and vow to make a good home for the baby and for Amy.

I awake in Recovery from a dreamless sleep. I need a drink of water, but my eyes feel too heavy to open and I'm too sleepy to talk. I hear the doctor tell me that I have a son and that the police are on their way. I fall asleep again and when I wake up I am in a room on my own with my baby asleep in a cot next to me. The walls are pale blue instead of grey, and the floor has light green and white tiles. Daylight filters through blinds that are the colour of pale custard. My baby is wrapped in a blue blanket, and I blink in wonder at all the colours. There is somebody in a dark blue uniform standing by the door, but thankfully there is still no sign of Edwin.

I try to sit up, but the morphine is wearing off and I feel pain from the stitches in my abdomen. The person in the uniform comes in closer and smiles at me. She's a police-woman and says her name is Faye Carter, and she asks if I'm up to talking. I manage to mouth at her that I need some water, and as I sip the cold refreshing nectar I look at my ba-by again. He definitely looks like a Jocelyn now, but I think I'll call him Joss for short. Amy will be tickled pink.

Amy. Where is my daughter? Is she hungry? Is she still crying for me? I come back to reality with a bump.

Faye sits down by my bed and says she wants to talk about the piece of paper I gave to the anaesthetist, and also about Edwin. She says my parents' address and my statement that I had been kidnapped checked out, and that the Missing Per-sons Team had contacted my parents, who are ecstatic and are on their way to see me.

My eyes fill up with tears that spill down my cheeks. So many nights I cried for my mother when Amy was sleeping and I didn't have to be strong for her. My greatest fear had been that they accepted I was dead and had given up searching.

I ask about Edwin, and Faye says he had been arrested as he waited outside the operating suite. He will eventually be charged with kidnap, kidnapping of a minor, and rape. However, he had no ID on him and had decided to remain silent and not give them his name or address, therefore as yet they have been unable to find Amy. My heart sinks, because I know Amy is his princess and he doesn't want her found. There is also the unspoken worry that the police won't believe me until they find Amy.

Faye asks how I travelled to the hospital. I reply that Edwin took me in his car, but made me keep my eyes closed. I tell her I managed to pull some fur from the car seat and gave it to the anaesthetist. She nods and asks me where I thought he might have parked his car, but all I can tell her is that when we arrived at the hospital I opened my eyes but it was dark and I didn't really take much notice of his car or where he parked it, as I was in too much pain and distress. She nods again and says the police now have the piece of fur and are searching the hospital car parks.

I tell her that he didn't need to carry me too far before we were at the doors of Accident & Emergency, and she assures me they will find the car very soon. I tell her the passenger seat will be laid down almost flat, and she speaks into her radio and passes the information on to the search team outside.

I can't believe what is happening to me. The two people I love most in the world apart from Liam and Amy come into the room. They have aged in the years we have been apart, and I break down completely at the sight of them. None of us can speak for the first few minutes. We hug together on the bed and they take a first look at their new grandson, completely oblivious to all the drama going on around him. They tell me he is beautiful, and that I am very pale but still beautiful. I smile at them through my tears and tell them they also have a 9-year-old granddaughter. Mum is lost for words again.

I want to ask if they know anything about Liam but can see Faye reappearing at the door, having kindly given us a few moments of privacy. She says a car with a passenger seat that is lying flat and covered with a greyish fur cover cannot be found in any of the hospital car parks.

He is one step ahead. He must have moved the car whilst I was in the operating theatre.

My joy is tarnished somewhat by the thought of my poor Amy still left alone in her prison, but at least Edwin is in custody and under lock and key himself. I ask what the next stage is, and Faye tells me Edwin's face is soon going to be on national TV to see if anybody recognises him.

Mum and Dad say we have a home with them as soon as I am recovered and out of hospital. I tell them the stay will only be temporary until I am able to stand on my own two feet again. Money in my bank account has remained untouched since 1987, and I can see my parents are getting older. I have no wish to interrupt their peaceful life with a child and a newborn baby if I can work and find my own place. Mum says it will all come with time.

I ask Mum about Liam, but she says they lost touch several years ago. She says she has no idea where he is, but tells me she will phone the Rachelle hospital and find out if he still works there. She tells me she is going to stay in the room with me all night.

When the nurse comes in to check my wound and bring milk for Joss I ask if there is a hairdresser in the hospital. She looks surprised, but says there is. I ask her to book an appointment for me.

CHAPTER 10 - AMY

MY HANDS ARE sore from banging on the door. I want my Mummy. Daddy took her away ages ago and she hasn't come back. I shout and shout, but nobody answers. Prince is in the house, but he's asleep on the bed. The duvet cover is all wet.

I'm hungry. I open the carrier bag that Daddy left and find a packet of crisps and a packet of Jaffa cakes. I put a crisp on top of a Jaffa cake and eat it; they taste a bit funny mixed together. I eat another Jaffa cake and then another one. Mummy says it's not good to eat more than three Jaffa cakes at the same time, so I delve deeper into the bag and see what else there is.

Daddy's put some fruit in the bag. I peel a banana and put the skin in the rubbish bin. He usually comes in with a black sack to empty the bin, but it's nearly full to the top with rubbish. I don't know where else to put the rubbish when the bin gets too full.

Prince wakes up. He's hungry too and cries. Daddy hasn't left him any cat food, so I give him a Jaffa cake but he sniffs it and turns away. I fill up my cup with some water and have a drink and give the rest to Prince. He laps it up with his tongue, but still cries for his cat food. I don't know what to do. I have another look in the bag but I can only see a loaf of bread and a packet of Rich Tea biscuits. I break one up and give it to Prince, but he's not very keen on that either.

Mummy left me some maths to do on the table. I've done the sums but I don't know if they're right. When she comes back she'll have to mark them with a tick or a cross. I don't often get many crosses because Mummy says I'm clever.

Will Mummy come and bring me something else to eat? There's nothing to put on the bread to make a sandwich except bananas or crisps. I've never had a crisp sandwich before, but I make one and it's quite nice. I wish Prince would eat one, and then he'd stop crying.

I pick up my reading book. I've already read it once before, but I like reading bits of it again. I like the bit where the children go down in the copper mine on the Isle of Gloom, and Lucy-Ann finds Bill Smugs' pencil in the cave. They think at first that he's the one bringing food to the miners. They explore the caves and Kiki flies off. Jack goes to look for her but the others are found by Jake and Olly, horrible men just like Daddy, and are locked in a small room that's the same as my house. They have a bolt on the outside of the door, just like me. They escape when Jake brings them food by pretending the air is bad and they can't breathe. Philip kicks out Jake's lantern and the three children run towards the main shaft just using their torches, trying to escape from the men. Jack was still lost in the tunnels and Philip, Dinah and Lucy-

Ann climb up the shaft and sail away, leaving Jack and Kiki behind.

Now why didn't I think of that? When Daddy brings food Mummy and I could pretend that we can't breathe, and then Daddy would have to let us out. I'm going to do that when I hear his footsteps coming. If I'd done that ages ago then perhaps I'd be on the outside now just like the children. Perhaps I'm not as clever as Mummy says I am.

When will Daddy be coming?

Philip goes to Bill's hut to ask him to help to find Jack, but Bill's not there. Philip finds some sort of radio in the hut and speaks to somebody on it who is asking for Bill. When Bill appears he tells Philip off for speaking on his radio. Philip says he's sorry but tells Bill that Jack is missing in the mines. Bill immediately starts speaking on his radio in a different language. He rushes out to his boat to go over to the island to find Jack, but somebody has damaged his boat and he can't sail it. They run back over the cliffs to find Joe's boat, but it is not there.

I'm tired. Mummy made the bed wet, but it's still dry underneath the duvet on my side. I get in but Prince is sitting crying by the door. I get out of bed again and have another look in the carrier bag, but there are only apples, a few Jaffa cakes, bread and Rich Tea biscuits left. I don't think Prince likes any of it. I break up another biscuit for Prince, but this time he eats it. He's really hungry. I give him some more water and he stops crying.

Mummy usually makes up a story for me before I go to sleep, but she's not here. Where is she? Will she be coming back for me? For the very first time I have to try and go to sleep without my mummy.

I sleep, but Prince wakes me up because he's crying really loudly by the door. There's also a funny smell. I think he's done a wee or a poo, or both. I can't see where he's done it, but it smells. Mummy will know where he's done it when she comes back.

Has the baby been born? Where is it going to sleep in our house? There's no bed for it, and it'll be too little to sleep with Mummy and me.

Where do cats do a poo? I tell Prince he has to sit on the toilet like me, but he's not listening. He's sitting by the door looking up at it and crying and crying. I think he's hun-gry again. I bang and bang on the door and shout, but no-body comes.

I'm hungry too. There are some slices of bread left and an apple, a banana, five Rich Teas and two Jaffa cakes. I give another biscuit to Prince, and let him drink out of my cup. I pick Prince up all the time now, but haven't even washed my hands since yesterday. Mummy would tell me off if she was here.

I eat two slices of bread and a banana. I fill my cup up with water again from the sink and drink the whole cup. I do a wee and clean my teeth and try to clean Prince's teeth with my toothbrush, but he doesn't let me and runs away.

There's nothing else to do but to read my book again.

Dinah runs off with Uncle Jocelyn's old book of Craggy-Tops, and Bill Smugs reads it and helps the children to find another secret passage from Craggy Tops to the Isle of Gloom that goes under the sea. He tells them that the entrance to the secret passage is at the bottom of their well, but above where the water is. Bill and Philip climb down the well and find the secret passage that leads them to the island, where they find Jake and Olly have locked Kiki in a cell, thinking Jack was in there as well, but he was crouched outside in the dark. Jack tells them that he has found a big machine where men are making piles of paper money that isn't real money, but people still spend it.

I've never seen any money. Mummy tells me you have to pay for things with money on the outside, but she says Daddy took her bag away with her purse in when she first came here. I would love to find big piles of paper money, then I could spend it on anything I want.

Bill Smugs tells the boys that he is a policeman who has been after the gang of bad men for a long time. He says that Joe is the one that brings them food in his boat and takes away the piles of money to their boss.

What an adventure the boys were having. Jake and Olly hear Kiki talking and open the door. She flew out and found where the boys were hiding, and they just start off down the passage back to Craggy-Tops when Joe appears with a gun and threatens to shoot them.

Does Daddy have a gun? Would he shoot me if I didn't do as said? I've never seen a gun, but Mummy has told me that it can kill people.

Joe locks Philip, Jack and Bill in the underground cave. They're all locked in like me again. Joe comes back to tell them the bad men are going to flood the mines with a big explosion, and that they'll be drowned, and then he locks them back in again. Bill opens the door with one of his spindly key things when Joe has gone, and they all escape.

Why can't I find a spindly key thing and open my door? Is it just grown-ups that have spindly key things? Has Mummy got one?

As they run up the secret passage they hear an explosion and the seawater runs in behind them. They wait until it fills up the well and then swim up to the start of the ladder, because the bad men had chopped away the bottom half to stop them climbing up. They see other policemen that Bill knew standing guard over the bad men and Joe. Bill tells them his real name is Bill Cunningham, and the policemen take the bad men away.

The children win lots of money for helping to catch the bad men. Jack and Lucy-Ann go to live with Philip and Dinah's mother, and everybody's happy.

All except me, I'm not happy at all. I want my mummy. Philip and Dinah have theirs, so why can't I have mine? I close the book but I don't put it down because I like to cuddle it.

I've eaten all the bread, and Prince has finished off the last Rich Tea. There's one apple left and two Jaffa cakes. Daddy needs to bring me some more food soon. Prince makes the house smell horrible. He cries all the time and keeps going to sit by the door.

I don't like apples, but I eat it because that's all there is once I have eaten the Jaffa cakes. Prince doesn't like apples either. I start to feel frightened because there is no food left in the bag. There is nothing else left in the house to eat.

I want to cry when Prince cries. I want my mummy. I cuddle my book and sit on the bed. The wet bit is drying out now, but there's a big stain. I don't know what else to do. I've read the book, eaten all the food in the bag, and there's only water left to drink. I give some to Prince and he stops crying for a while.

I think that maybe if I lie down and go to sleep, then Daddy will be here when I wake up with my breakfast. I lay down and Prince comes and lies on the bed with me. I can hear him purring and I can feel his warm body.

I wake up in a panic because I can't see anything. Prince is still asleep beside me. The light bulb has broken again, and Daddy needs to put a new one in. I begin to cry because I don't know where the torch is. I can't even see to go to the toilet. I cuddle Prince in the dark and wait for Daddy to bring me some breakfast. Nobody comes.

I cry and cry, and all my tears make the pillow wet. Prince jumps off the bed and I think he goes over to the door again, but I can't see him. I cuddle my book close to me. It's all I have left.

CHAPTER 11

JESSIE LLOYD SIPPED some Earl Grey tea in her new conservatory and looked around appreciatively. Outside the snow lay thick on the lawn, but inside she was cosy and warm. The builder had done a wonderful job, and she was pleased. She would be able to buy some nice wicker chairs and get some cushion covers and matching curtains. She im-agined herself sitting by the door in the summer and watching all the grandchildren playing in the garden.

She would certainly recommend the builder to her neighbours. Iris and George had come in to have a nose about, and now they wanted a conservatory too. Mr Evans had been polite, tidy, and very thorough, and he had cleaned up any mess he had made straight away. He had even been tidier than her dear departed Artie had been, God rest his soul.

She took her empty cup through to the kitchen, and then walked into the lounge and switched on the television. There was never much worth looking at these days; too much sex and violence and shouting. Why didn't they put on a nice musical to cheer people up? Didn't people watch musicals these days? Jessie thought not; people were all too busy watching other people having sex or bashing each other over the head with iron bars.

A soap opera's dreary theme tune assaulted her ears as Jessie tut-tutted with annoyance. She pressed the remote control and decided to have a look at the crime programme on the other channel. The chap that presented it always seemed such a nice man, and it was more interesting than that awful soap. Jessie didn't care who was bedding whom; sex had long since lost its fascination, and she'd rather have a nice hot dinner these days anyway.

She'd missed the first ten minutes, but the chap with the nice smile was giving out a phone number for anyone to call who could give the police details of the man in the photo they were putting on the screen.

Jessie took a look at the photo and nearly fell off her chair in surprise.

The man on the screen was Mr Evans, the tidy builder who had done such a good job with her conservatory.

CHAPTER 12

THE OLD LADY had been correct, and she had even kept hold of Evans' recent invoice and receipt. One of the keys on Evans' large key ring fitted snugly in the Yale lock, and the front door swung open. Inspector John Hatton could hear no sounds at all inside the house, and as his eyes looked to left and right he wondered where would be a good place to begin the search.

"Shall I look upstairs first, Sir?" WPC Faye Carter was already making her way to the stairwell.

"Yes, that'll be a good start. I'll look down here." Hatton tried the first door off the hallway, which led into the lounge. He was struck by the cleanliness and order; no book was out of place on the shelving, and CD's and DVD's were stored in racks in alphabetical order. Cushions were plumped up on the sofa, and the carpet was clean and had been recently vacuumed. There was a bureau in one corner containing his business cards and headed paper, lists of customers, and invoices to be paid. Everything seemed in order, right down to the vase of dust-free artificial flowers on the dining table. As he went back out into the hallway he realised what had been bugging him about the lounge; there were no family photographs lining windowsills or in frames upon the walls.

He tried the kitchen, which was just as clean. There were no dirty plates in the sink, and no food left out on the work-tops. Even the cat's bowl on the floor full of dried food looked as though it was regularly washed out. Hatton looked around for a cat, but assumed it had gone out through the cat flap in the back door. He saw a type of American walk-in fridge and thought it rather large for somebody living on his own, and was surprised at the amount of food in the fridge, and also in the cupboards and on shelves in the little pantry he found near the kitchen. There was even another larger American-type fridge in a corner of the pantry.

WPC Carter stuck her head around the pantry
door. "Nothing upstairs Sir."

"Ok, but let's have a look at this." Hatton wondered why a man living on his own would want to put a bolt on the outside of the fridge door.

He slid the bolt back and opened the fridge door. Instead of the usual milk, rashers of bacon and margarine he could see steps going downstairs to some sort of cellar. There was a light switch just inside the door, and Hatton switched it on. There was a strong wooden door in front of him at the bottom of the stairs. Hatton went down the steps with WPC Carter following behind. He tried the handle, but the door was locked.

Fishing in his pocket he brought out Evans' key ring and tried the first key. As he fiddled with the lock he thought he could hear a cat mewing on the other side of the door. Finding the correct key at last he opened the door and a cat shot past him and up the stairs.

Hatton tried not to gag at the stench of shit and cats' piss that hit him as he opened the door. He tried but could not see too far into the room from stairwell's dim light.

"I'll go and get a torch from the car."

Faye Carter ran back up the stairs and reappeared with a torch. Hatton shone it around the room and as he did so he could see a young girl sitting up on the bed, shielding her eyes from the light. She began to choke.

"Daddy? I can't breathe! The air is bad! You have to let me out!"

"Amy?" Faye Carter ran over to the girl. "I'm here to help you. I'm a policewoman. My name is Faye, and I'm going to take you to your mummy."

Faye held out her hand to the little girl, who clutched it as though her life depended on it.

"Are you asthmatic? Are you having trouble breathing?" Faye did her best to comfort the girl while Hatton investigated the rest of the room.

"I copied Philip, Dinah and Lucy-Ann. It's how they escaped." Amy's breathing returned to normal as Faye checked the rest of the bed.

"Were there other children in here with you then?"

"They're in here, in my book." Amy pointed to the book next to her under the duvet. "I've done a wee and a poo on the bed. Will Mummy tell me off? Daddy needs to change the light bulb and I couldn't find the toilet. I'm so hungry. I ate all the food. Prince is hungry too."

"Nobody is going to tell you off, darling. There's food for Prince upstairs. Do you have any other clothes?"

Faye could see the girl had taken off her lower garments and was half naked under the duvet.

"Our clothes are kept in a drawer under the bed."

"I'm going to take you upstairs to the bathroom. You can have a good wash and a change of clothes, and then we're going to make you something to eat and then take you in the car to see your mummy."

Faye was happy to leave Inspector Hatton looking around the fetid cellar. She had no wish to stay down there a moment longer than she needed to. Holding the terrified girl's hand she led her up the stairs and into Evans' kitchen. After she had adjusted to the light, she could see the girl's eyes were as wide as saucers, taking in everything around her.

"That's a clock isn't it? My mummy told me about clocks. They tell you what the time is." Amy pointed towards the kitchen wall with her free hand while still managing to hold on to her book.

"That's right. Have you never seen one before?" Faye wondered how long the girl had been incarcerated.

"Daddy wouldn't let us have one." Amy stopped in her tracks and pulled Faye over to the window.

"I can see through this. Is it a window?" She pulled the net curtain back. "Is that outside? Is that the Isle of Gloom?" Faye wondered what on earth the girl was talking about:

"Yes, you can see through the window to the street outside. That's a green area opposite with the big tree in the middle. Children can play there."

"Is Philip sitting under the tree?" Amy could hardly bear to drag herself away.

"Who's Philip? Come on, we need to get you washed and dressed upstairs." Faye was conscious that the girl was still half naked.

"He found the bad men making paper money."

"What bad men? Where?"

"In here." Amy held up her book.

"Oh."

They climbed the stairs, with Amy's head still swivelling from left to right.

"Is Mummy up here?"

"Mummy's in hospital. This is Daddy's house. We'll see Mummy soon with the new baby."

"What sort of baby is it?"

"He's a boy; your little brother."

"No. Mummy says he's my stepbrother because we have different daddies." "Why is Daddy's house so big?"

"Most houses are this big, Amy."

"Mine isn't."

"It wasn't your house. It was a room in Daddy's house."

"We didn't have any windows in our house."

Faye's eyes pricked with tears, and at that moment she hated Evans with a passion that was increasing by the minute. She found his pristine bathroom irritating: as she began to run the bath for Amy she lifted the toilet seat up, pulled the towels onto the floor, and unfolded the flannels.

"Who is your daddy then?" She helped Amy to undress completely, but then noticed the look of terror on the child's face.

"I can't swim! I'll drown in the sea!" Amy backed away towards the far wall.

"It's a bath, Amy. It's not the sea. You won't drown because you're a big girl now."

"Mummy washes me at the sink."

Amy was shaking her head and Faye decided it wasn't worth upsetting the child any more.

"Ok. I'll help you to wash at the sink if you like?"

"Yes please."

Faye pulled out the bath plug and filled up the sink. "Who is your real daddy then, Amy?"

"I don't know, but Mummy says he's called Liam Darrah and that he's a doctor who looks after children. I've forgotten what the word is."

"A paediatrician?"

"Yes, that's it. I can nearly spell it. Mummy said I only left out the first 'a'."

"That's very good." Faye sponged the girl all over and dried her with one of the towels. "I don't think I can spell it."

"Mummy teaches me. She's very clever. She's a doctor as well."

Amy was dried and dressed by the time Hatton found his way upstairs.

"Do you like salmon, Amy?"

He didn't know how anybody could have stayed in that cellar for more than one day and remained sane. He was filled with admiration for the little girl and her mother.

"Yes. Daddy brings us salmon sometimes."

"I've opened a tin of salmon and made you some salmon and cucumber sandwiches. There's plenty of crisps as well."

"I'm really hungry."

"Come downstairs then, and have something to eat."

"Where's Prince? When can I go outside?" Amy had managed to eat three sandwiches in record time and a bag of crisps.

"Prince has gone out. Somebody will come back for him later on. You can go outside in a minute. We'll have to find a coat for you though, because it's very cold outside."

Hatton had a look inside the ground floor cloakroom, but could find nothing suitable for a 9-year-old girl.

"Why is it cold?" Amy's curiosity knew no bounds, and Hatton wondered how long she'd been cooped up in the cellar.

"It's winter, Amy. Have you never seen snow? How long have you been here?"

Amy chewed on a wine gum as she spoke.

"Mummy says I was born on the bed in our house. I've never been outside."

Hatton wanted to pick the little girl up in his arms and show her the world, but right now Bingley Road in Woodside would have to do as a starting point.

"I'll tell you what, Amy. Would you like to wear my jacket when we go out?" Faye looked at Amy and was rewarded with a smile as bright as sunshine.

"Yes please, I'd like that."

"What about shoes? Where are your shoes, Amy?"

"What are shoes?"

Amy looked blank until Faye pointed to her own.

"Daddy never brought us any shoes. We always wear socks on our feet. I have lots of socks."

"Don't worry. I'll carry you over the snow. It'll be too cold and wet for your feet without shoes." Hatton closed his eyes momentarily, took a deep breath, and clenched his jaw in anger.

CHAPTER 13

"WHAT'S THAT WHITE stuff falling down?" Amy snuggled close to Hatton and held her book close to her chest. With her free hand she reached out and tried to touch the unfamiliar, wet substance that melted as it fluttered down onto her skin.

"It's snow, darling. Some children like to play in it and build snowmen, but others prefer to stay indoors." Faye had never known a child ask so many questions.

"I want to play outside in it."

"Mummy will have to buy you Wellington boots to keep your feet dry first."

"Can we go to Mummy now?"

"Of course. We're going in this police car." Faye opened the car door and Hatton deposited Amy carefully on the back seat.

Amy touched the leather seat and looked out of the window.

"I'm outside but I'm inside."

Faye laughed as she did up the child's seatbelt.

"Yes, and we'll soon be inside the hospital where Mummy is."

"Will I see Daddy there as well?"

"No. You're not going to see Daddy for a long time."

Faye felt the evidence in the cellar would keep Evans away for hopefully the remainder of his life."

"Oh good, I want to see my real daddy instead. Where's my real daddy?"

"We don't know, but I expect Mummy will try and find him soon."

As Hatton started the engine Amy clutched her book tightly to her.

"Am I having an adventure like Philip, Jack, Lucy-Ann and Dinah?"

"Of course you are. It's even bigger than theirs."

"Wow!"

"Hey – I used to read those books when I was your age!" Hatton smiled as he changed into second gear. "They're the ones with Kiki the parrot aren't they?"

"Yes. Kiki can talk and understand what Jack says."

"Good old Kiki. I always wanted a parrot as a kid." Hatton laughed.

"So do I, but I don't think Mummy does."

As Hatton approached the hospital he could see a couple of his colleagues at the front entrance, and wondered whether the Press had already got wind of the story. He hoped for Amy's sake that she could be reunited with her mother before the flashbulbs started popping and the whole story exploded in their faces.

Picking up the child he was pleased to see the pavements around the hospital had been gritted. He wondered whether it was for the patients' benefit or to stop them taking legal action if they slipped over on the ice. He rather favoured the latter.

Treading carefully towards the front entrance, he saw PC Ford come towards him.

"The Press are on their way. There's not much time left. I'll head them off here as much as I can. Roberts is on the back door."

"Good man. Is the mother still on the maternity ward?"

"Yeah. It's locked apart from visiting times."

"Get Greenslade outside the ward. We're going to need some backup."

"You don't need to carry me now, the floor's not wet."

Hatton smiled and set the child down. Amy, overawed to be in such a large building, suddenly took hold of his hand. The small warm fingers in his suddenly reminded him of all the times when he hadn't been there to hold his own children's hands. Margaret always took great pains to constantly remind him of the fact.

"We're going up in the lift, Amy. Mum's on the seventh floor."

The lift doors swung open and Amy bolted towards the front entrance.

"Amy!" Faye was instantly on the alert and running after the fleeting child. "Come back! We can go up the stairs if you want!"

She caught up with the child and gave her a cuddle.

"I'm not going in there. No, I don't want to!" Tears had filled the girl's eyes and she was panic-stricken.

"You don't have to go up in the lift. Come on, I'll walk upstairs with you."

Faye and Hatton trudged up the stairs with Amy holding Faye's hand. She had calmed down by the time they reached the entrance to the maternity ward. Hatton spoke through the intercom, and the door opened automatically.

"Where's Mummy then?" Amy looked around and then looked back at Faye.

"She's in the side room; over there. Off you go, and we'll wait outside."

Amy peeped around the door to the side room. She saw a lady sitting up in bed feeding a baby with a bottle of milk. Another lady and a man sat nearby.

"You're not my mummy!" She ran back out into the corridor. "Faye, that's not my mummy in there!"

"Of course it is. Come on, I'll show you."

Faye opened the door again.

"Excuse me Dr Nichols, I just wanted to make sure it was you, and that they hadn't moved you off somewhere else."

"Thank you so much for finding her. I don't think she recognises me now."

Beth smiled as she finished feeding the baby. She sat him up ready for winding. Faye held out her hand towards the child.

"Come in Amy. Yes, it's Mummy but she's got a different haircut."

Amy took another look at the lady on the bed and then rushed over and climbed up to sit by her mother's side. Beth gave the baby to her mother and wrapped her arms around her daughter.

"I'm so, so glad to see you!"

"Why have you cut all your hair off?" Amy looked at her mother in surprise. She hardly had any hair left at all.

"I didn't want it anymore. This is called an elfin cut. The hairdresser put the plait in a bag for me."

"Can I see it?"

"Yes, but see your brother first."

"You said he's my stepbrother."

"Well, he is. But think of him as your brother. We have a lot to thank him for."

Amy walked over to where Sally Nichols sat holding her grandson.

"Hello. You look like Mummy."

"Hello Amy. I'm your grandmother. That means I'm your mummy's mummy. This man is your grandfather."

Amy looked up at her grandparents and smiled, and then peered at the little red, screwed up face contorted with rage at having his feeding bottle taken away.

"He's ugly!"

Beth laughed and enjoyed the first sight of her daughter standing there with her grandparents.

"He'll pretty up as he gets older. Do you know what his name is?"

"What?"

"Joss. That's short for Jocelyn."

"Jocelyn's in my book! He's Philip and Dinah's uncle!"

"Well, this is a different Jocelyn. He's your little brother. Joss doesn't know it yet, but he's a very special baby. He saved us having to spend any more days and nights with Edwin. We must take great care of him."

Amy stroked her brother's cheek.

"Thank you for saving us, Joss. Thank you very much."

CHAPTER 14 - LIAM

THE RAIN FINALLY decided to splatter the sidewalks as Dr Liam Darrah made his way along Elm Street, downtown Toronto. Ducking into The World's Biggest Bookstore to avoid a soaking he was soon lost among the familiar book-shelves, but that afternoon his gaze eventually wandered to the British newspaper section. He liked to glance through The London Times once in a while; somehow the English place names made him feel closer to his father, still living alone in the wilds of Norfolk. Every time he took Patty with him to visit they never seemed to get along, but then he re-membered that most people usually rubbed his father up the wrong way. The only person he'd ever seemed to get along with was Beth, but that was a long time and many tears ago.

He picked up a copy of The Londoner Standard; it would be something to read on the tram back to Queen Street. When the rain stopped he walked briskly towards the tram stop, the newspaper rolled under his arm.

As usual the tram was full of shoppers with bulky purchases, workers hurrying to get home, and tourists. There were a multitude of accents and he picked out the flat vowels of a family from somewhere in the North of England on the seat in front of him, making their way back to their hotel after a day out at the CN Tower and the Eaton Center. He'd become quite proficient at recognising the British regional accents when he'd worked in Norfolk; at first they'd all sounded the same, but then as his ears had become accustomed to the variations in sounds he had found the different pronunciations quite delightful.

One of the British children was a toddler of around 18 months, who looked about the same age as his own son. He stood up on the seat and looked around, until admonished by his mother. Liam smiled at the mother and then decided to unfurl his newspaper for something to do. He quickly read the headlines which were a couple of days old, but then the sounds of the people around him fell away as he gazed in stunned silence at the picture inside the front page. The photograph caused him to miss his usual stop, and when he did look out of the window he found he'd ended up much further down Queen Street than he wanted to be.

The photograph showed a slim woman with very short blonde hair on the steps of a hospital in Croydon, Surrey. She looked very pale and tired and somehow overawed. She was accompanied by a nurse holding a newborn baby in a shawl, and by a young girl of about 9 or 10 years of age dressed in clothes that were slightly too big for her. Both the woman and the girl were wearing sunglasses even though it was January, and the girl was clutching a large book close to her chest. With them were an older couple possibly in their early to mid sixties. The older couple he recognised immedi-ately as Sally and Robert Nichols, the two people who would have been his mother and father in law had Beth lived.

He took a closer look at the woman wearing sunglasses. She looked older than when he had last seen Beth, but she had Beth's mouth and fair hair. He did not recognise the young girl at all. He supposed her children must be brother and sister; fathered by her abductor.

The second page of the newspaper was mainly devoted to a story by Iain Treacher of how a Mr Edwin Michael Evans had lived the quiet and proper life of a builder and architect in Bingley Road, Woodside, South London, for a number of years. The neighbours had all described him as a bit of a loner who used to keep to himself. However, his social misfit tendencies were to hide the fact that for almost 10 years he had kept a young woman, Dr Elizabeth Nichols, prisoner in his cellar, along with her daughter Amy whom Dr Nichols had delivered herself with no medical aid.

Liam's heart pounded in his chest with the realisation that Beth was the woman in the photograph, and that she was still alive. He suddenly felt nauseous and needed to get off the tram. When it came to a stop he staggered off and ex-pelled the remains of his lunch onto the sidewalk. He was conscious of people staring at him, but at that precise mo-ment he did not care at all.

It took him a while to get back to his house on Kingston Street, but the extra walk cleared his head. Keeping the pre-cious newspaper under his arm he stopped in one of the stores along Queen Street to buy some cold water. The shop assistant had asked him if he was ok, and Liam just nodded; lost for words.

He could see on his return that Patty had already given Toby his dinner. The toddler sat contentedly in his high chair gnawing on a piece of apple, as Patty ate her meal beside him.

"You're later than usual today. Have you already eaten in town?" Patty smiled, but then her expression changed as she turned to look at her partner.

"Yes." The lie came easily.

"Are you ok? You look pale."

"I think I ate a bad hamburger, eh?" Liam kissed the top of his son's head and gave Patty a peck on the cheek.

"I take it you don't want anything to eat?"

"Not yet; I'm going to have a shower."

As the jet of warm water pounded on his face Liam tried to come to terms with the item of news that he had read on the tram; that his previous fiancée whom he thought had died was actually still alive and had been held prisoner for almost a decade. There was also the question of the little girl in the picture; the writer stated that Amy was the daughter of Dr Nichols, who had been delivered whilst her mother had been held captive.

Wrapping himself in a towel Liam padded out of the en-suite shower room and had another look at the photograph in the newspaper lying on the bed. It was difficult to see whom the girl resembled due to her wearing sunglasses, but he wondered whether there was a possibility he could be her father instead of the abductor. He also knew that he could never rest until he found out.

He felt sick all over again. He sat on the edge of the bed and put his head in his hands.

"Oh dear, you are ill aren't you!" Patty popped her head around the door on her way to bath Toby.

"Sorry baby, I'll be alright in a minute. I'll read Toby a story when he's had a bath."

"Ok, but you're making the quilt all wet."

Liam stood up to dry himself. He put on a t-shirt and a comfortable pair of jeans, walked through to his son's room, and sat down in the rocking chair and put his head back on the cushion. Only a few hours ago his life was well ordered and predictable; off he would travel to his downtown practice every morning, and at the end of the working day he would return on the six o'clock tram. Patty would have a meal ready, and they would sit and eat together with their son. Af-ter Toby was asleep they would watch TV in the evenings, and sometimes they would make love on the sofa if the programme sucked.

His life had suddenly been turned upside down. He looked around his son's bedroom; the little cot in the corner crammed with soft toys, the rocking horse that Toby loved to sit on, and the bookshelf next to him full to the brim with well-loved and well-thumbed books. He had a son whom he adored and cherished, and a beautiful red-headed partner that most guys would give their right arm for. However, Patty wasn't Beth, but she was the mother of his son and he would do anything for her. The only thing he couldn't do was to love her as much as he'd once loved Beth.

Liam smiled as he listened to Toby's protestations at having to lie still for a clean diaper. Patty seemed relieved to hand him over to his father.

"Hey, little man! Which story tonight then?"

Liam gathered his son in his arms in the rocking chair and reached over for a few books. He let Toby choose a story, enjoying the clean baby smell and warmth of the little body close to his.

When the stories were told and Toby's head lay heavy on his chest, Liam closed his eyes and rocked quietly in the chair.

He knew he could never give up the love he felt for his son in favour of a possible daughter that he had never known existed. On the other hand he had loved Beth with a passion so deep that it had taken nearly eight years for the memories of her to begin to fade enough to let somebody else into his life. That somebody else had been Patty, who to date had no idea that Beth had ever existed, and not even the first inkling that she, Patty, would always be second best.

The baby slept on his chest, sucking his thumb. Liam stood up, laid his son in his cot, and covered him with the quilt lovingly stitched by Patty. He put on the night-light and went downstairs to his study, switched on the computer, and searched on the Internet for Iain Treacher's email address at The Londoner Standard. The message he sent informed the journalist that he was once engaged to Doctor Beth Nichols, there was a strong possibility that he could be Amy's father, and that he had no idea where Beth or her parents were now living. Just for completeness he wrote a letter to Beth, care of Iain Treacher at the Londoner Standard, and mailed it that evening.

Iain Treacher, already sniffing out a front-page story, did not take very long to reply. By the time Liam had returned home from work the next day there was a message informing him to prepare for a trip to the UK.

CHAPTER 15 - LIAM

THE TIME HAD come to tell Patty; there was no way around it. Iain Treacher had contacted the hospital where Beth had stayed, and had asked the ward manager to contact Beth's parents at the address in Suffolk they had provided. He had forwarded Liam's letter to the ward manager to send on. Liam had given permission for his email address to be handed over to Beth's mother and father, and Sally Nichols had replied to the erstwhile son in law she had not seen since the early days of Beth's abduction. Iain wanted a front-page story and was prepared to pay for it. Liam had informed him that any money must go to Beth if she was prepared to cooperate.

On receiving Sally's email two days later, Liam waited until later that evening when he and Patty were cuddled together in bed.

"I'm going to have to take a week off work and fly to the UK, baby."

He kissed the top of her head and closed his eyes, waiting for the inevitable response.

"Why?" Patty lifted herself up on one elbow and looked down at him.

"There's something I need to show you." He reached over and opened his bedside cabinet, taking out the newspaper. "Have a read of page two." He lay back down on the pillow while she read, all the time watching her face for any change of expression.

Patty read the article and folded up the newspaper.

"I don't understand. Who is this Doctor Beth Nichols? Do you know her then?"

She lay back down and moved closer to Liam, placing one arm across his chest and one leg across his thighs.

"I was engaged to her many years ago, but I thought she was dead. I have to find out if I am the father of her daughter."

Patty stiffened beside him and she sat up again.

"My God! You never told me this!"

"I only just told you because I thought she was dead. I never knew she'd been abducted and kept prisoner."

"How could you not tell me? Am I so unimportant? Well what about Toby and me? Can we come with you?"

"I don't think that would be a good idea."

"Do you still love her?" Tears were already starting to fill Patty's eyes, and Liam hugged her.

"You are my partner now. I stopped thinking about Beth when I met you. We have a beautiful son together. I just have to find out if I have a daughter or not as well. I hope you understand."

The constant drain on his emotions over the past few days had left Liam feeling washed out and exhausted. He switched off the bedside lamp as Patty turned over on her side away from him. He cuddled up to her back and slipped an arm around her waist.

"I'm so sorry, baby. I really thought she was dead. This is the first news I've had about her in nearly ten years."

"You should have told me."

"I know. I'm sorry. I just thought it was all over and I pushed it to the back of my mind."

"Will you come back to us?"

"Of course. There's no question of that. If I have a daughter I just need to see her and get to know her."

"We'll be waiting for you, Toby and me."

"I know, baby. I know."

Liam also knew that Iain Treacher would be waiting for him at Heathrow airport. He supposed the man was probably on the case now; booking his flight and hotel rooms for both of them and the inevitable photographer while he and Patty slept into the small hours. There was no going back now.

Patty was unusually silent at breakfast the next day as she spooned cereal into Toby's mouth. After breakfast Liam checked his emails and came back into the kitchen.

"I just have to go downtown and see a couple of patients at the clinic, then I'll return at lunchtime to pack. There's a flight leaving at 8 o'clock tonight. Iain Treacher has booked me on it."

"When will you be back?"

"My flight comes in at 3.30 on Saturday afternoon. Why don't you and Toby come down and meet me? We can show Toby the planes; he'll love it."

"Yes I'd like that."

"Ok. See you soon then. Can you order me a taxi for about four o'clock baby, eh?"

He kissed her and brushed the top of his son's russet curls with his lips. The baby stopped chewing momentarily to flash him a big smile showing a few pearly white teeth caked in cereal.

"Yes; reluctantly." Patty gave him a thin smile as he turned towards the front door.

CHAPTER 16 - LIAM

HE HATED AIRPORTS. All the waiting around and wasted time made him irritable. Liam sat at one of the tables outside the Swiss Chalet restaurant at Pearson International airport eating roast chicken and watching the people go by. He knew he was too wound up at the thought of seeing Beth again to get any sleep on the plane, and figured it was going to be a long night. Treacher would be waiting for him at the other end; flashbulbs would be popping, and his mind was too distracted by the recent events to even think about concentrating on a book for the length of the journey.

After his meal he visited a gift store in the departure lounge and bought a pad of writing paper with a cover depicting the CN tower. He decided to compose another letter to Beth during the flight; it would occupy his mind and channel his thoughts in the right direction.

When his flight was announced over the loudspeaker Liam made his way to the gate and waited in line with British tourists returning home after the Christmas vacation. His ear quickly attuned to the accents and he wanted to tell them about Beth and scan their faces for a response, but figured they had probably not kept up with any news from home during their stay in Toronto and would not know what he was talking about.

Walking past the checkout staff on the gate, he stepped onto the plane and made himself as comfortable as he could in his seat for the seven-hour flight. He felt a strange excitement at seeing Beth again and meeting the girl who could possibly be his daughter, but at the same time felt guilty at leaving Patty and Toby. He momentarily closed his eyes and pictured his son's beaming smile that morning; the deep love he had for his child would ensure a return to the land of his birth, but he could not help but feel as though he was floundering in a sea of uncertainty.

"Hello. I'll try not to be any trouble."

Liam came back to reality as an elderly British lady strapped herself into the seat next to his. He smiled as he adjusted the clips on his own belt. He hoped she didn't intend to talk non-stop the whole time.

"Hi. You'll be fine I'm sure. I'm Liam." He pretended to take an interest in the air hostess as she pointed out the emergency exits.

"Pleased to meet you Liam. I'm Shirley. I've just said goodbye to my son and his wife. No matter how many times I do it, it never seems to get any easier."

"I've just done the same, although my son just a baby I'm still going to miss him dreadfully." Liam smiled again at the fading memory of Toby in his high chair that morning.

"Of course. Will you be visiting relatives in England? Are your parents English? You have a very slight British ac-cent on some words." Shirley turned to look at Liam, her interest growing in her new travelling companion.

Liam took out his notepad and pen, hoping to immerse himself in his writing.

"Yes, I'm going to visit my father. My mother is Canadian and my father is English, so I have dual nationality. I lived in England with my father for a few years while I was training to be a doctor. They're divorced now but seem to get on better than they ever did, now that they live on separate continents."

He hoped the part-lie would quell her curiosity. The engines started up and the plane began to move forward to join the queue for take-off. Liam looked at the blank sheet of paper and wondered what on earth to say to Beth, the only woman he had ever truly loved.

"I'd say your wife is a very lucky lady. Some men can't be bothered with babies and toddlers. My husband only took an interest in Anthony when he was about 18 and they could go off drinking together. You obviously miss your son. It's lovely."

Liam smiled again at the old lady as the engines roared and the plane began to gather speed down the runway. He'd been so excited about meeting Beth again that he hadn't even thought about visiting his father, who had no idea he was on his way to the UK. As the plane took off he hoped he'd be able to speak to his father before he saw his son's face plastered all over the newspapers.

Taking advantage of a lull in the conversation after dinner as his travelling companion dozed, Liam found a pen in his jacket pocket and opened his writing pad.

What could he say to somebody that was once so dear to him that it took eight years just to begin to expunge the memories? Liam sighed and chewed the end of his pen in concentration.

My dearest Beth,

I don't know if you received the last letter I sent you, so I'm writing another one.

If I had passed up buying the Londoner Standard in a bookstore in downtown Toronto a few days ago I would never have seen your photo inside the front cover. The fact that you are still alive makes me happy beyond my wildest dreams.

We had the world at our feet ten years ago. To have you snatched from me at the time was devastating, and for many years I felt that I could not go on as the grief was too raw. After five years I stopped working in the UK and went back home, hoping the new environment would help me forget. I moved back with Mom and slowly took up the fragments of a new life.

Patty is part of my new life now, and we have a beautiful son, Toby, who is 18 months old. I am very thankful for Patty; she took on somebody too damaged to function properly, and turned my life around. I look at her and feel nothing but admiration. She organises my life and takes care of our son. I come home after a day's work to a well-kept house and a happy, smiling toddler.

However, I can never feel for Patty what I felt for you. You were my soul mate; my other half. We could finish each other's sentences. When I held you in my arms I felt complete. I want you to know that I still have that piece of paper with a heart on which you drew and left on your pillow the day you were taken. Patty has never found it, nor will she ever do so.

I realize of course that now we are two different people. What you have gone through is catastrophic, and I would not be surprised if you never wanted to look at a man again.

We cannot change what has happened or turn back the clock. I could no more leave my son than fly off to the moon, and there's no way I would ever take him from his mother. Patty loves me with all her heart, and she has made me the man I am today; able to cope and function again. I suppose what I am saying is that although I will never stop loving you I cannot be the husband you once wanted me to be. I don't know if you still think of me as your fiancée, but too much has happened in the meantime and I am a different person now.

My darling I am so looking forward to seeing you, albeit just for a short time. Please accept me with all my imperfections.

Truly yours,
Liam xx

He tore off the pages carefully, folded them in half, put the letter in his jacket pocket and closed his eyes.

He must have dozed for a while. When he awoke the stewardess was serving coffee. Shirley passed him a steaming cup and he drank gratefully.

"You had a nice snooze there. Pleasant dreams?" She took out a bag of food from behind the seat in front of her. "Would you like a biscuit?"

Liam rubbed his eyes as he drained the small plastic cup.

"I guess. I don't really remember. Thanks for the cookie." He yawned and smiled.

"They're chocolate hob-nobs. I always take some wherever I go."

"You're a star, Shirley; a true star."

"I think they'll dim the lights soon so that we can have a few hours sleep. I always find it hard to sleep though when I've just said goodbye to my son and his wife and children."

"I don't think I'll be able to get much more sleep. I'm too wired."

"Looking forward to seeing your father?"

"Well, it's a bit more than that. I'm going to see Dad, but also I'm meeting up with somebody else that I haven't seen for a very long time."

"That must be very exciting. I always feel like that on the outward journey to see Anthony and Clare. Are they waiting for you at Heathrow?"

"No I don't think so. She's just had an operation. I don't think she's up to travelling much at the moment."

"I hope she's not too poorly to see you." "So do I Shirley. So do I."

The lights dimmed as the plane flew into the night. As Shirley stood up to find the washroom Liam settled back into the seat and closed his eyes again. He listened to the noise of the engines and was grateful for the chance to be alone with his thoughts for a while.

Dawn was breaking when he awoke. The other passengers were stirring and looking out of the windows. Shirley was reading with the aid of a small spotlight shining down from above her seat.

"There! You did manage to sleep. You looked very peaceful. I only wish I could have grabbed a few hours."

"I was tired. I've been awake a lot the past few days."

"Thinking about your young lady no doubt." There was a twinkle in Shirley's eyes as she turned to look at him.

"Yes. I must admit. Beth has been in my thoughts night and day."

"You must love her very much."

"It was a long time ago. We've both changed and moved on now though."

"Not by the sound of it from what I can tell."

Liam laughed and took a cup of coffee from the stewardess.

"You're too shrewd Shirley!"

"I know a young man in love when I see one."

"It's not that simple. I'm with somebody else now. We have a young son."

"Ah. I see." Shirley put down her book and sipped her tea. "All I can say is don't do what I did. I stayed for years with a person I didn't love, just for the sake of my child. I ended up hating the sight of him. Follow your heart. If it leads you across the Atlantic, then follow it."

"Thanks for the advice. It's not that I don't love Patty, I just love her in a different way to the way I love Beth." He bit into another chocolate hob-nob.

"No woman wants to know she's second best. When Patty finds out there'll be hell to pay."

"She won't find out."

"Hmm. My guess is that she probably already has an inkling." Shirley nodded sagely and opened up her book again.

Liam sighed and tried to summon up the appetite to eat the frugal breakfast handed out. As the plane approached Heathrow and he felt the landing gear descend, he wondered if Iain Treacher was already waiting for him.

CHAPTER 17 - LIAM

WHEELING HIS SUITCASE into the Arrivals hall, the first thing he spotted was his name written in red ink on a large piece of card, held by a man sporting the kind of designer stubble that to Liam looked as if he had just rolled out of bed.

"Are you Treacher? Hi. I'm Liam Darrah."

"That bastard's still sleeping it off. I'm Paul Fraser the photographer. Pleased to meet you."

The two men shook hands and Liam followed Fraser out of the airport building.

"We're in the short-term car park. I've booked you into the same hotel as us near the Nichols' family home in Norwich. It'll take about 3 hours to get there, so if I were you I'd get some shut-eye on the way."

"Does Beth know I'm coming up?"

"Yes but don't worry, we'll give you two some time alone and then Iain will take some notes for the article if he's awake, and I'll take some photos. We've got the exclusive, so there's no rush. You'll be able to have a shower and get some kip first."

"Kip?"

"Sleep."

"Uh-huh. I want the money to go to Beth."

"Iain's sorting it out."

The inside of Fraser's Range Rover was a jumble of camera equipment and folding ladders. Liam found an empty corner to stow his suitcase, and soon Fraser was expertly negotiating the rush hour traffic on the M25.

"So when was the last time you saw Dr Nichols then?" Fraser turned onto the M11 and Liam cast his mind back.

"May 20th 1987. We were both doctors working in the emergency room. Her shift finished at 10pm, but mine was only just starting. I asked her to ring for the night porter to escort her, but she said she'd be fine. It was only a five-minute walk back to the accommodation. If only I could turn back the time."

"We'd all like to do that, mate. Iain's spoken to her; she's really excited for the chance to be able to meet up with you again. Sally Nichols had even rung the Rachelle hospital to find out if you were still working there."

"What did they say?"

"No-one had heard of you."

"It was a long time ago." Liam yawned and settled back against the headrest. "Is it still only seven thirty in the morning?"

"I told you. Get some kip. I'll give you a nudge when we get there."

When he awoke he saw road signs indicating the way to the centre of Norwich. Memories came flooding back of himself and Beth that last Christmas, walking around the main shopping mall with their arms around each other. He'd bought her some warm pyjamas with a mistletoe motif on the front; she always complained the bed was too cold when he worked the night shift. She'd bought him a pair of Santa socks com-plete with sleigh bells. He could still see her curled up on the bed, laughing at him standing in front of her wearing nothing except the socks and a huge grin.

Fraser pulled the Range Rover into an expensive-looking hotel, whose frontage was covered in ivy.

"We're here now. They have a good restaurant if you want something to eat." He turned off the engine.

"Great, but my body clock's a bit out of step at the moment." Liam unwillingly brought himself back to the present, collected his suitcase, and followed Fraser into the hotel's lobby to check in. He felt he could sleep for a week.

"Your room's next to mine. I'll give Iain a knock and see if he's up."

The floorboards creaked with age and there was an aroma of sausages and bacon along the maze of passageways that led to the bedrooms. Liam looked towards the door to his room that Fraser indicated, and then waited to see if Iain Treacher responded to the knock.

There was no answer.

"I'll give you a shout in a couple of hours and then we'll have something to eat. I'll have that lazy bastard up by then."

Liam smiled and entered his room. It was clean, and the bed looked inviting. After showering and shaving he lay down and sank his head into the soft pillow, and was asleep in minutes.

It was as though he had only just dozed off when he was awoken to the sound of knocking seemingly coming from afar. As Liam came back to consciousness he was aware that somebody was rapping on the door of his room. Covering the short distance from bed to door with legs that Beth had often likened to two long sticks of celery, Liam came face to face to face with the grim reality that was Iain Treacher after a night out on the piss.

"Paul's ready for lunch now. I'll have a shower and join you later. It's nice to meet you by the way. I'm Iain." He held out a clammy hand.

"Good to meet you. I'm ready to eat too."

Liam shook the proffered hand and acknowledged the photographer standing behind in the passageway. As he withdrew his hand and looked at the dishevelled state of the journalist, he wondered whether he should wash it again before he ate anything.

There was a buffet laid out temptingly in the restaurant. Liam found he was quite hungry and tucked in to a full roast turkey lunch with all the trimmings.

"As soon as Iain's down we'll go over to the Nichols' place. We'll drop you off there; the grandparents are going to take the kids out, and then we'll come back again when you two have had a chance to meet up."

"Thanks. You've definitely got the exclusive, but Beth and I need to talk first."

"Absolutely. We wouldn't want to intrude straight away. Iain'll find a pub somewhere I expect, but I'll try and keep him on the orange juices."

Liam laughed and sat back in his chair, replete.

"Ok. I take it that Beth knows I'm coming?"

"Sure. We've been in contact with her parents. She's looking forward to seeing you."

"The feeling's mutual. I'm getting quite nervous now; I wrote a letter to her on the plane."

"You'll be fine. I sent off your other one. We look forward to a good story when she's read the letters."

Iain appeared as Liam and Paul were finishing their coffees.

"All ready to go then?"

Liam could see Iain had managed a wash and shave, and had combed his hair. He looked altogether much cleaner and more presentable.

"Yep. Let's do it." Liam's heart began to turn somersaults in his chest, and he checked inside his jacket pocket to make sure the letter was still there.

It was just a short drive to the Nichols' bungalow situated on a quiet tree-lined cul-de-sac. Liam stepped out of the Range Rover and waved goodbye to his acquaintances.

"Give us a couple of hours. See you soon."

"No probs. Have a ball, mate." Paul drove off as Liam walked up the garden path and rang the bell.

CHAPTER 18 - LIAM

THE WOMAN WHO opened the door was Beth, and yet she wasn't the Beth that Liam had waved goodnight to ten years before. His first glance took in the extra few lines on her thin, pale face and her ultra-short elfin haircut. He quelled an impulse to take her into his arms. When he looked in her eyes they were wary and guarded, and not the ones that had tenderly gazed back at him from their bed that last morning after lovemaking. He stood on the doorstep, mute and overawed. She smiled at his awkwardness.

"Hello Liam. Come in. I've been expecting you."

Beth stepped aside to allow him to enter the hallway, and then closed the door to the outside world.

"It's so good to see you." Liam's voice sounded unnaturally husky.

"Come in and sit down. I'm a bit slow I'm afraid. I've not long had a caesarean and I'm still in a bit of pain."

She moved like a person forty years older down the hallway and into the lounge, and sank down gratefully into a cream leather settee. Liam thought it best to give Beth her own space, and perched on the edge of another matching two-seater settee.

"What can I do to help you?" He was at a total loss for what to say to this stranger who sat stiffly opposite.

"Nothing really. Just seeing you again makes me feel better already." She smiled again and shifted in her seat to get more comfortable.

He could not take his eyes off her. The new haircut made her look even more fragile and ethereal.

"Are you well otherwise?"   *What has that bastard done to you?*

"I'm okay. I'm still getting used to being free again and seeing other people. I don't think I'm quite up to shopping along the High Street yet though." She gave a rueful laugh.

"Were you angry that I'd contacted the Press? I saw your photo in the newspaper, but didn't know how to go about finding you other than emailing the person that had written the article. I sent off a letter to you via the newspa-per. Did you receive it? I also assumed your parents wouldn't still be living in their old place. I couldn't remember their address."

"No I never got the letter, but that's not to say it won't arrive. My parents moved several years ago into this retire-ment bungalow. Luckily for me there's three bedrooms. Amy still wants to sleep with me at the moment, but hopeful-ly with time she'll be happy in her own room."

The question he had been burning to ask could not be held back any more. He took a deep breath and hoped for the best.

"Tell me to mind my own business if you like, but is Evans Amy's father as well?" He held his breath as he waited for the response.

"No, Liam. You are. I had suspected I was pregnant, but I hadn't had a pregnancy test. After I was abducted it was obvious, but to keep Evans happy I let him think Amy was his. However, she's the image of you. You'll meet her later when Mum and Dad bring her back." She stated it mat-ter-of-factly, unaware of the effect of her words.

Liam put his head in his hands and a huge gulping sob escaped from his body. To be the father of a ten-year-old child who was unaware of his existence was more than he could bear.

"Some fucking paediatrician I am. I couldn't even take care of my own daughter!" He wiped the tears from his eyes and put his arms around the woman he loved as she moved across to sit beside him. "Forgive me that I wasn't there for you." He tried unsuccessfully to stem a fresh river of tears.

"Nothing was ever your fault Liam. He knew I was working late shifts that week, and he was waiting. He stalked me and I was a sitting target. I thought he was a bit weird when I treated him in A&E, but hey, what's done is done. I'm free now." She sighed and sank her head into his shoul-der.

"I live in Toronto and have an 18 month old son. His name is Toby. He has red hair the colour of leaves in the fall." He sniffed and closed his eyes as he held Beth tighter in his arms.

"I'm glad you found happiness with somebody else. You deserve it."

"It took me eight years to even start to forget what we had, but if I thought you had still been alive I'd have waited forever."

"You weren't to know. Mum said the police did what they could at the time. They searched for years, but everyone eventually assumed I'd been murdered."

"I want to kill that bastard; bollocks to the Hippocratic Oath."

"Then you'd be a prisoner and he would have ruined both of us. No; let him rot in his cell and think about what he's done."

They sat in silence with their arms around each other, wanting nothing more. The chiming of the grandfather clock in the hallway told Liam that almost two hours had passed in the blink of an eye.

"Mum and Dad will be back soon, and then the journalists. We need to make ourselves pretty."

"You are pretty. I even like your new haircut."

"It's the new me; older, wiser, and a sensible mother of two."

"How's the little fella?"

"He's beautiful. I've named him Jocelyn; Joss for short."

"Unusual name."

"He's an unusual baby. Amy gave me the idea for his name. He freed me from my prison. I looked his name up and it says people called Jocelyn have a desire to inspire others to a higher cause."

"I wish I was his father."

"Every time you visit Amy you'll get to know Joss. In time he'll come to think of you as a surrogate father, I'm sure." Beth stood up with a slight grimace of pain. "I'm going upstairs to have a quick wash. Make yourself some coffee. Mine's milk and two sugars please. I'm not breastfeeding, so can eat and drink what I like."

"You didn't want to breastfeed?"

"No. I couldn't do it. I have to have some control over my body again. It's a psychological thing I suppose."

"I can understand that." His jaw clenched in anger at what she must have gone through.

"I've been offered counselling, but want to deal with it in my own way."

"Of course. You were always mentally stronger than I could ever be. God knows how you've got through the last ten years."

"I thought of you often, and I had to be strong for Amy." She smiled at him as she made for the stairs. "Back in a minute. It's so lovely to see you again Liam."

He took the opportunity to rinse his face under the cold tap as he waited for the kettle to boil. In a short while he would meet the daughter he had never known he had. What on earth was he going to say to her?

CHAPTER 19 - LIAM

THEY SAT IN companionable silence drinking their coffee. When the key turned in the lock Liam stood up. He smiled at Sally and Robert Nichols as they came into the room. Sally wheeled the baby in his pram, and Liam tried hard to catch Amy's eye as she hid behind her grandfather.

"Liam! Wonderful to see you!" Sally stepped forward and gave him a hug.

"Hi Sally. I'm still reeling from the shock!" Liam kissed her and shook Robert's hand. Amy ran to sit beside her mother on the settee.

"Amy, where are your manners? Say hello to Liam. He's your real daddy."

Beth looked down at Amy, who stood up again and smiled, clutching a book to her chest.

"Are you the doctor who looks after children?"

"Yes, Amy. I'm so happy to meet you." "You
talk funny."

"I live in another country a long way away. I came over here on an aeroplane to see you."

"Do I call you Liam, or Daddy?"

"Whatever you want is fine with me." He saw himself in the child's face; the eyes were his own eyes.

"Can I call you Liam then?   I think it's better than Daddy."

"Of course you can.   I'll come and see you as often as I'm able to.   I'll take you on days out and we'll get to know each other better."

"I'd like that."

Amy took hold of Liam's hand as the baby began to cry.

"Come and see my little brother. His name is Jocelyn, the same as Philip and Dinah's uncle."

"Who are Philip and Dinah?"

Liam's heart melted as he felt Amy's warm hand in his. He fought to stave off a fresh well of tears threatening at the back of his eyes.

"They're in here." She held up a book. "We don't call him Jocelyn though; he's Joss for short. Do you want to pick him up out of his pushchair?"

Liam looked around towards Beth.

"Sure. Give him a little cuddle. He'll like that."

"He's a fella. Us boys all like cuddles."

Liam grinned as he held the baby. He saw Joss had Beth's mouth, but was darker in colouring. The baby stopped crying and looked at him with eyes that were several shades darker than Beth's light grey ones. *His eyes.*

"He's recently had a bottle. He just needed a cuddle." Sally took off her coat. "Liam, can I get you anything to eat?" "No, I'm fine thanks. I had lunch before we left the hotel."

"Where do you work now?" Robert looked fondly over at the man he would have liked to call his son-in-law.

"I have a clinical practice in downtown Toronto. I've been building up the practice for the last few years. I only live a short tram ride away. We live in an area known as The Beaches; close to the stores, but also close to the shores of Lake Ontario."

"It sounds a lovely part of the world."

"It is. My mother also lives close by; she's remarried now."

"Will you be seeing your father while you're over here?"

Beth remembered David; a Norfolk man born and bred, with a heart of gold that held a soft spot for her.

"Yes, but I've been so caught up in events that I haven't got around to phoning him yet."

"You can use our phone in the study and let him know you're here."

"Thanks. I'll do that when the journalists have gone. I think they might have arrived now."

Robert went off to answer the doorbell, and showed Treacher and Fraser into the lounge. After introductions were made they stood about awkwardly until Sally reappeared.

"Here's some tea and biscuits for you all. I'll take Amy into the kitchen as it's getting near teatime. Beth, do you want me to take the baby?"

"No, I'll hold him, Mum. I think he's asleep again now anyway."

"Ok. Give me a shout if you need anything."

Liam settled next to Beth on the two-seater settee, and Treacher and Fraser sat opposite. The journalist switched on a small voice recorder and put it on the table between them.

"You don't mind if I record our interview? It saves me trying to decipher my terrible handwriting afterwards."

Liam looked at Beth, who shrugged and snuggled the baby in the crook of her arm.

"It's ok with us."

He put a protective arm around her, gave her shoulder a squeeze, and waited for the first question. It was not long in coming.

"How long had you known each other before the abduction?"

Treacher directed his question to nobody in particular. Liam waited for a few seconds and then took up the story when Beth failed to answer.

"We were friends at medical school, and had started dating about a year before Beth was taken. I was living in the UK with my father at the time, who had just split from Mom. The course of our lives were set; we would train to become consultants, get married, have lots of babies, and live in a country cottage with roses around the door."

"Well, you got to be a consultant anyway." Beth smiled and looked down at Joss.

"Dr Nichols, are you finding it difficult adjusting to normal life?"

Beth took her eyes from the baby to look at Treacher.

"I must admit I haven't been out much because I'm still recovering from a caesarean birth. At the moment I can't think about going shopping or anything like that. I expect it will come with time, but the outside world just seems too noisy and fast-paced for me after being imprisoned in a basement and just seeing the same two people for ten years."

The journalist nodded and nibbled on a biscuit.

"Dr Darrah; do you think you might come back to live in the UK permanently?" Treacher had asked the one question that Liam hoped he wouldn't have to answer.

"Although I have dual nationality, my partner is Canadian and she would not want to be uprooted. I have a young son and a thriving paediatric practice in Toronto. My life is back in Canada, but I will make frequent trips to the UK in the future to see my daughter." His words sounded dull and lifeless. Liam felt Beth stiffen in his arms.

"How did you feel when you found out you had a daughter?"

Treacher was trying his patience, and suddenly Liam wished he'd never got the Press involved.

"The same as you'd feel under the same circumstances I expect; a mixture of shock, happiness, and anger and frustration at not having the chance to have been part of her formative years." His answer was abrupt. He felt Beth move closer to him to give support.

"How has your partner reacted to the news?" The journalist was digging deep into his emotions, and Liam hoped the money being paid to Beth would be worth all the anguish.

"She was upset that I hadn't mentioned anything to her before. We searched for years, but eventually we all thought that Beth had been murdered, and I had tried to put it all behind me when I eventually moved back to Toronto."

"Dr Nichols; how do you feel knowing that Dr Darrah will be flying back on Saturday?"

Liam pulled Beth closer to him, and there was a moment of silence while she gathered her thoughts and feelings.

"I was a prisoner for a long time. Liam built another life for himself in my absence. I wouldn't have wanted him to grieve for the rest of his life. He has moved on and so must I. I am still a relatively young woman, and now I have the chance to build a life for my children and myself. When I am stronger I want to re-train and work again and support my children. I feel as though I must not hold Liam back. He must go back to his partner, his son and his life. He will always be welcome to see Amy and maybe even take her to Canada for a holiday, but at the end of the day he has his life in Toronto and I have my life here in the UK." She reached over the baby to pour herself a cup of tea.

"Are you going to testify against Evans at his trial?" Treacher took another biscuit.

"Of course. I want him put away for the rest of his life."

"What are your feelings towards him?"

"Anger at depriving me of my freedom for so long, and fear of what he might do to me or Amy if he is ever released."

"How did he come across to you?"

"Definite mental health issues; loner, misfit, and probable drug addict. From something he once said I think he'd also been abused as a youngster. That doesn't mean though that I'll ever forgive him for what he's done."

"Dr Darrah. How do you feel towards Evans?"

"How do I feel towards the person who kept my fiancée prisoner against her will, abused her physically and sexually, and probably damaged my daughter for the rest of her life? How do I feel? What a stupid fucking question!"

Liam's voice shook with anger and he closed his eyes. Beth laid her head on his shoulder, stopping him in his tracks from striding over to Treacher and punching his lights out.

"Can I take some photos?" Fraser interrupted to smooth over the tension in the room.

"Fire away. I can't promise we'll be smiling though." Liam looked at his watch and wondered how much longer he would have to endure the torture.

"I'll take some of just the two of you, and then if you want to bring Amy in I'll take a few more of Dr Nichols with the children and then yourself with Amy."

"Fine. Just get it over with."

"We'll be on our way soon. You have the hotel room for the rest of your stay, but we'll be gone tonight. We have the cheque to give you today."

Liam stopped short from outwardly cheering. He nodded curtly.

"Thanks. Give it to Beth."

The baby was hungry and told his mother of the fact in the only way he knew how. Fraser had taken enough photos to fill a small album. Sally Nichols showed Treacher and Fraser to the front door and then returned to take the baby.

"I'll feed Joss and change his nappy. You two sit there and recover. We'll be in the kitchen for a while longer."

"Thanks Mum." Beth sighed and handed over the baby to her mother, who made a tactful exit.

Liam still sat on the settee with his arm around Beth. He felt shell-shocked and unwilling to move. Beth's body was warm against his, and for a few minutes they enjoyed the peace and silence.

"Thank God that's over. If I still smoked I'd have a cigarette now." Beth grimaced and let her arm fall across Liam's shirtfront.

"Abduction and imprisonment; what a way to cure yourself of a nicotine addiction! I'd better not recommend it in medical circles though."

Liam laughed a somewhat hollow laugh and let his lips touch the top of Beth's head. The scent of her hair brought back a thousand memories.

"I'm going to see Dad tomorrow, but I'll come and see you all the following day before I have to fly back."

He tried to block out the pleasurable feel of Beth's body against his. Somehow it felt so right being there and holding her; he didn't want to think about going home.

"He'll be so surprised to see you and to hear what's been going on."

"He always liked you. Unfortunately he and Patty rub each other up the wrong way."

"Yes I remember the old boy could be a little bit cantankerous. I just used to smile at him a lot." Beth laughed at the memory.

"He loved you. I loved you." Liam sighed and buried his face in her hair. "I still love you. I never stopped loving you." His eyes filled with tears. "Oh God, what a fucking mess!"

CHAPTER 20 - BETH

I'M KEEPING A diary as I try to adjust to my new life. It's so wonderful to know what the date and time is again.

Wednesday January 17th 1996 7.30pm

The midwife comes to see me every day. Joss is gaining weight, as he should. All I had for Amy was my own milk, but I can't put Joss to the breast this time. It just doesn't feel right.

The midwife will stop coming soon and the health visitor will take over. I'm told that I'm doing very well considering, but inside I feel I'm coming apart at the seams. I can't face even taking the baby for a walk in his pushchair at the moment. The outside world seems so noisy, with cars beeping their horns and thousands of people rushing about everywhere. The sky is huge. Amy seems to be adapting well as children tend to do, and today she even forgot to carry her book about with her. She's learning to use a knife and fork. The time is right to prepare her for starting school.

Liam flew back home to his partner and his son and broke my heart all over again. He gave me a letter that he'd written on the plane coming over here. It said it all really. I know I must stop thinking of him in a romantic way. Patty was waiting for him at the airport with Toby, and there is no place for me. I will see him when he comes to collect Amy in the school summer holidays, and I must be thankful for that. I know he loves me deeply, just as I love him, but the situation we're now in only succeeds to drive us further apart.

Mum and Dad are my port in a storm. They help with the children, and try to encourage me to venture outside. The money I received from the newspaper is enough to allow me to put a sizeable deposit down on a property of my own, but I need to retrain to be able to work again in order to pay off a monthly mortgage. I don't feel strong enough mentally at the moment to be able to do that. The days flow by one into the other, and I sit in my parents' lounge and look out of the window, or explore the world from the safety of Dad's office computer.

Dad set me up with an email account and I think he must have given Liam my address, because he sent a message to say he'd landed safely back in Toronto, and that Patty and the baby had been waiting for him at the airport. I know I shouldn't have replied, but I did. I sent him an email to say how much I'd enjoyed seeing him again. It had taken 10 years to be able to look into his eyes, but the thought of Patty and Toby waiting for him to come home put a different slant on things for me. I'd played the scene in my head thousands of times of what I'd say to him and what I'd do when we fi-nally met up, but in the end I didn't do or say any of it. Liam belongs to somebody else now, and I couldn't bring myself to tell him how much I loved him.

He wanted me to go with him to visit his father, but I didn't want to go out of the house and leave the children with my parents. I could tell he was disappointed to be going without me, but it was probably for the best anyway.

You would think I'd be ecstatic and on cloud nine at being released, but after seeing Liam I feel terribly low and am having trouble feeling hopeful for the future. Liam was my future, but that's been snatched away now. I feel I have to try and continue to be strong for my children, but the ground has fallen away from under me. Mum thinks I need antidepressants, but I don't really want to get hooked on those. The world and his wife are on Citalopram, but I told Mum it was only the baby blues and it would go away when my hormones settle down.

Sunday January 21st - 7.55 pm

I'm pressing Amy's new school uniform ready for tomorrow. Mum took her to Norwich yesterday and she came home very excited holding her new skirts, blouses, shoes and blazer. She's turning into a typical girl; she loved her shopping expedition and wanted to know when she could go again. I can't believe how quickly she has adapted.

Mum has enrolled her in a small private school that is only about 20 minutes walk away. I feel guilty at the cost of it, but Mum and Dad say it's the least they can do to make up for lost time with their granddaughter. There are only about 10 children in each class, and I know this will be better for Amy as she is bright and will be given work appropriate to her level. There won't be the disruption, hustle and bustle of hundreds of children in a big school, and I will miss her terribly. I've only been separated from her for a couple of days when Joss was born, and the thought of her going off to school is not aiding my depression. I keep catastrophising that Evans will escape and kidnap Amy all over again. The headmistress knows of Amy's situation, and to start with she will only be going to school in the mornings and will gradually build up to the whole day after a few weeks.

I hang Amy's uniform on the outside of her wardrobe and sit down on her bed and cry. She's reading a new book that Mum bought her in Norwich, and I need to say goodnight and switch the night-light on. I cry a lot these days, but I don't know if it's losing Liam that's making me cry, my post-partum hormones, or the thought of my daughter going off to school tomorrow.

Amy sits up and cuddles me and tells me not to be sad. I smooth down her lovely long fair hair and rest my head on hers. I know I cannot hold her back and keep her with me forever, but she brings sunshine to a life that I feel I'm losing control over. I kiss her goodnight and switch the nightlight on, as she hasn't yet got over her fear of the dark. She's so excited about starting school and says she won't be able to sleep. I check her half an hour afterwards but there is no sound.

By the time I have given Joss his last feed of the day Mum and Dad are also asleep. I can't settle and decide to go downstairs to the office and turn on Dad's computer. There is a message from Liam.

Dear Beth,

Many thanks for your email. Dad was disappointed not to see you. I think he still has a soft spot for you. He says you're always wel-come to take the children and visit. He says he'd like to meet his grand-

daughter. If you don't feel up to visiting him, can he come to your parents' house? Have a think about what you'd like to do and let me know.

I feel as though I've left a part of me behind in Norfolk. I feel strangely unsettled now and keep thinking back to when I held you in my arms. There was so much I should have said to you on that last day, but the time flew by so quickly.

I hope Amy enjoys her first day at school tomorrow. Tell her that I'll be thinking of her, and that I'll call her often.

Would Robert mind if we used his phone to keep in touch? I'll also start to send you more emails, now that your dad has shown you how to use the computer. Technology never stands still does it? Emails are so easy; as you can see, there's really nothing to it, and it'll be cheaper than using the phone all the time. It'll be a great way of keeping in touch. One day I think people will use emails all the time instead of sending letters!

Love and hugs,
Liam xx'

Monday 22nd January – 10.12 am

At 08:26 I'd put Joss in his pushchair and set out with Mum and Dad to walk Amy to school, but at the end of our road I had to turn back. My heart was pounding in my chest, and I'd started to sweat even though there was ice and snow on the pavement. The sky seemed endless and grey, and stretched for miles into the far beyond. The world was too big; the cars too noisy, and my legs were shaking. I kissed Amy and walked as quickly as I could with the pushchair back to the bungalow. Dad wanted to come back with me, but I told him to stay with Mum and Amy.

I cuddled Joss on the settee and cried with fear at what was happening to me. I was a supposed sensible well-educated 36-year-old doctor. I took stock of my situation and reasoned that I was still recovering from the birth and that my muscles were probably too weak to walk about after ten years in captivity. I put to the back of my mind the terror I felt at having to go outside.

Mum and Dad returned minus Amy, but said how happy she'd seemed when they'd left her in the classroom. Mum asked if I'd like to walk back with her at lunchtime to collect her from school, but I immediately started to feel panicky again at the thought. I told Mum I felt tired and that I'd have a nap on the settee whilst she was gone. Mum said Amy had asked if I could be there when she came out of school.

I truly did want to be there for my daughter, but my heart started pounding again, knowing I'd have to face the outside world. For years I'd lived in my concrete prison yearning for the day when I could step outside, and now I had the chance I couldn't do it. I knew I'd have to make a superhuman effort to be able to walk away from the house for 20 minutes to meet Amy, and I also knew I just wouldn't be able to accomplish this. The fact caused tears to sting the back of my eyes, and I held on to Joss tighter on the settee. Dad sat down next to me and asked if I was ok, and I re-member mumbling something to the effect that I was fine.

While Joss had his mid-morning nap I re-read Liam's email. I also asked Dad whether he minded if I phoned Liam from time to time. Of course he said he didn't mind at all, but in the long run he said it would be cheaper to communi-cate by email. I decided it was time to embrace the new technological age:

Dear Liam,

Dad helped me set up with an email account, but he doesn't mind us using the phone from time to time. Emails are a good way for Amy to keep in touch with you, although if she actually spoke with you it would be better I think. What is the time difference? Are you five hours behind the UK? If so you would have to call at weekends I expect when you're not at work and Amy is home.

Of course your dad can come and see Amy any time he likes. I don't feel up to going out and visiting just yet, but he is welcome here. Amy started school today; she's only there for mornings at the moment, but I expect will soon feel able to stay all day.

We both left many things unsaid, but I think it's probably better that way. We are two different people to those of ten years ago, and there's no way I would want to interfere with the life you have now.

Love and hugs back,
Beth x'

I watched the blue line going across the screen as the email was being sent, and wished I could have told Liam how much I loved him and how much the thought of seeing him again had kept me going through the dark days of imprisonment. I wished I could have told him that there would never be a man who could even begin to match up to him, and that losing him all over again to another woman had made me start to wonder whether life was really worth living after all.

Surprisingly within a few moments Liam had typed a reply. I checked my watch and it was 10:47am. Across the pond it was very early in the morning. Liam had always hated mornings:

'My dear Beth,

I'm here in the office while Patty and Toby are still in bed. I'm not sleeping too well lately, and I can't stop thinking about you. I can't wait to talk to you and hear your voice again. Perhaps we can make a regular time to talk?

More love and hugs, Liam. xxxxxx'

Wednesday 24th January – 11:54 am

It's getting harder to come up with excuses not to walk with Mum when she takes Amy to school. It's getting to the point where I don't even want to open the front door to put the empty bottles out for the milkman. The sky seems vast and unforgiving. The wound from the caesarean is healing nicely and I'm not in so much pain now, but the thought of venturing outside into the great wide open sends me into a panic. Poor Amy has had so much to cope with in her short life, and to see her mother having a full-blown panic attack in the street would really freak her out I'm sure. I feel sweaty and shaky at the thought of having a panic attack in front of everybody. What if I can't breathe? What if I'm sick?

try and reason with myself that I'm just panicking about having a panic attack, but it's no use. Mum's getting suspicious that there might be something wrong with me. She wants me to make an appointment to see a GP at their practice just to get checked over, but I could no more go outside and walk to the surgery than I could walk to the school. I'm frightened. I think I'm losing my sanity.

The doorbell rings, but Mum and Dad have gone to pick up Amy. My heart thumps as I peer around the front door, and I try not to look up at the sky. The postman hands me a parcel and I close the door quickly. It's the web-cam!

I send an email to Liam to let him know I read his message, but I assume he'll be getting ready for work. I cuddle Joss and sigh, as the day stretches endlessly before me. I know I will have to wait until at least 11pm to receive a reply.

'Darling Beth,

I can't wait to speak to you again. I'm still sleeping really badly, and Patty is getting used to me walking about at night and getting up early. I want to call you from here in my office at 05:45 my time (10:45 your time) every morning before I go to work. Will you be at home then (I hope so!)?

How is Amy getting on at school? Is she staying for the whole day yet? Please could you email me some photos of yourself and Amy?

See you tomorrow.

Love, hugs, and more love than you could ever imagine. xxxx'

'My dear Liam,

It's late at night now for me. I've taken some photos of Amy in her school uniform today, and have attached them for you. She's adapted so well that next week she'll be staying at school all day. The headmis-tress told Mum that Amy is ahead of her classmates in maths, reading and science, but will need to catch up with German and classics (my two worst subjects at her age). It's a wonderful school; last night she brought home a flute and played a little tune on it. She's surprisingly musical, given that I don't play any instrument and sing like a corncrake. It must come from your side of the family.

I am at home all the time at the moment as I'm having a few problems going outside. I haven't mentioned it to Mum and Dad as I don't want to worry them, but the thought of walking Amy to school brings me out in a cold sweat. I yearned for the day when I would be free, but now I am I find I'm still in a kind of prison of my own making. I am trying to reason with myself but it is just not working.

I'm so looking forward to talking to you on the phone. Of course I'll be here to receive your call.

Lots of love,
Beth xxx'

Thursday 25th January 11:18am

An email has popped into my inbox.

'My darling Beth,

It was so wonderful to talk to you just now. I couldn't sleep at all last night and by all accounts should feel like shit now, but I'm still on a high. Patty must have woken up and wondered where I was. She came into the office and found me sitting at my desk at 05:20, patiently waiting for the right time to phone you.

Thanks so much for the photos of Amy. I still can't believe I have a daughter; she's so beautiful. Could you get Sally or Robert to take some photos of you and send them to me in your next email please?

I'm worried that you're having trouble leaving the house. Maybe it's post-natal depression? You know as well as I do that an anti-depressant will help. Do it for me; go to the doctor and get checked over.

I can hear Toby crying. I will say goodbye for now and will speak again tomorrow.

I love you,
Liam xxxxx'

My heart skips a beat at his declaration of love. I want to feel his arms around me, holding me close. However, I know this is never going to happen, and that I will just have to make do with seeing him on screen. Life is so unfair.

Mum comes into the office and asks if I would like to go with her to a jewellery party at a friend's bungalow opposite. She says we can take Joss and go on from there to pick Amy up. I immediately start feeling panicky at the thought of going outside and crossing the road, let alone walking to the school. I shake my head and Mum knows there's something going on. She gives me a hug and I cry as though my heart is breaking.

I tell Mum through my tears that I'm frightened to leave the house, and I find the confession brings me some small relief at getting the problem out in the open. Mum asks if I would like the GP to come and see me at home, and I nod. What's left of the sensible part of me knows I have to try and fight these overwhelming feelings of fear and anxiety somehow, before they totally take over my personality and reduce me to a gibbering wreck confined to rocking backwards and forwards on the settee.

Dad appears and offers to phone the GP, and the doctor agrees to come to the house after his morning surgery. I feel dreadful at putting everyone to so much trouble, but Dad says I have been through a lot and it is going to take me a while to adapt to my new life. Both Mum and Dad are surprised at how well Amy has settled down, but I know that children quickly learn to adjust to new surroundings. I only wish that I could do the same.

Mum lets the doctor in on her way out to pick Amy up from school. I am grateful that she takes Joss with her in his pushchair. I tell the GP I'm sorry to bring him out, and start to cry again. He says it's no trouble, and Dad fills him in on the recent events. After examining me the doctor says I'm recovering well from the birth, but am suffering from severe anxiety and depression. He prescribes 10mg of Citalopram to be taken at night, and says it will take a couple of weeks before it kicks in. I'm to let him know if there's no improvement after a fortnight, and he will consider increasing the dose. He also says not to suddenly stop taking it if I feel better, but to stay on it for a few months and then gradually wean down.

Saturday 27th January 16:24pm

Amy was over the moon at being able to speak to her daddy. She played the tune on her flute to him that she'd been rehearsing all week while I held the phone up. He emailed a photo of himself, and I've printed it out and put it in a frame by Amy's bed. She's a different child; she's adapted well to sleeping in her own room and only has occa-sional nightmares. She no longer constantly clutches the reading book that Evans gave her, and it now seems perma-nently consigned to one of the shelves in her bedroom.

When I spoke to Liam before he went to work yesterday I was aware that at one point Patty must have been in the room with him, as he stopped speaking and suddenly ended the call, and I had to wait a few minutes until he re-dialled. I asked if Patty had discovered him talking to me, and said that I didn't want to cause any trouble between them. He replied that he wasn't committing any crime, and who he talked to on the phone was none of Patty's business.

I've just realised that I haven't felt like crying at all today. I still don't feel like going out to the shops or taking Amy to school, but apart from a bit of a dull headache I have not felt too badly all day. Perhaps the Citalopram is starting to work? I remember that many of my past patients were taking anti-depressants, and now so am I. I tell myself it's nothing to be ashamed of.

I decide to send Liam an email later on that day.

'My dear Liam,

Amy was so delighted to speak to you today. She now has the pho-to you sent in a frame by her bed. I think I'll take another copy of it and do the same! I'm attaching one of me that Dad took today.

I'm not so weepy today on the Citalopram. I'm hoping that soon I'll feel like going outside. I'd love to take Joss out in his pram, but I suppose I'm trying to run before I can walk. Joss is a very contented baby and I suppose I'm very lucky in that respect.

Just to be able to speak to you in the mornings is a real tonic for me, but please stop calling if Patty doesn't like it. She mustn't feel threatened by our past relationship. However, we have a child together and she must understand that you would want to keep in touch for that reason. The last thing I would want to do is break up the little family that you have now.

All my love,
Beth xx'

Sunday 28th January 07:19am

Liam must have stayed up late last night, as there is a reply to my email when I log in before breakfast.

'Darling Beth,

Thanks so much for the photo. I'm glad to hear you're feeling a little bit better. Depression creeps up on you and you don't realise it until it's got you in a firm grip.

I will continue to talk to you every morning before I go to work as long as you're agreeable. I can't start my day now without hearing your voice. I can't help my feelings for you. I loved you long before I met Patty, and I will continue to love you until the day I die. I will never stop loving you.

Patty is my partner and the mother of my son, and I love him with all my heart. My conflicting emotions are tearing me up. I will never love Patty as much as I love you, and there is absolutely nothing I will ever be able to do about it. Sometimes I just want to jump into a plane and take up where we left off, but to hear Toby call me daddy as he reaches out his arms for me is just the most wonderful thing in the world. He is relying on me to love and provide for him, and I cannot let him down. I only wish I could have got to know Amy sooner. I feel I ought to be there for her as well, but cannot be in two places at once. I have set up a direct debit so that every month you will receive enough money to cover her school fees and whatever else she needs. I'm so sorry but that's all I can do, apart from hopefully seeing her in the school holidays if she (and you) would like that.

Yours forever,
Liam xxxx'

I put my head in my hands after I read the email. My love for Liam was like a deep ache that wouldn't go away. I wanted him so badly at that moment that it was like a physical pain, and I knew the only way to remove the agony was to be held in his arms. I just had to reply with a message of my own.

'My dearest Liam,

Thank you so much for the direct debit. Of course you can see Amy whenever you want to. She is so very happy to have found her real daddy at last.

The love we had was a beautiful thing. The wonderful memories I had of you have stayed in my mind all throughout the last ten years. I cannot expunge you from my memory no matter how hard I try. I ache to be with you; it is a gnawing ache that will not go away. However, the love you and your son have for each other cannot be tarnished in any way; I do not want to break up your family. We have to be content with talking to each other on the phone, and I look forward to this every day. I know Amy is counting the hours until she can speak to you later on.

You will stay forever in my heart.

Beth xxxx'

Within a short time an email comes back.

'My darling Beth,

I can't sleep for thinking about you. It 2:30am here and I've already told Patty I'm coming back to bed. She's not happy that I'm sitting here in the office sending emails in the dead of night. She heard us talking on the phone last week, and I think she's going to make it very difficult for me to actually be able to get some free time to talk to you. She's starting to appear in the office whenever I'm in here, so for the next few weeks or so I'll email you from work. That doesn't mean I'll not be able to speak to Amy; she's ok with that, but she's not happy that I'm spending so much time speaking to you.

I have to go now. Love you. xxxxxx'

Wednesday 31st January 09:31

Today I managed to walk with Mum, Amy and Joss to the top of the road without breaking into a cold sweat. Mum carried on taking Amy to school, and I walked back to the bungalow with Joss in his pushchair. I took a little plastic bag in case I panicked and felt sick, but I was surprised to feel quite normal in that I didn't feel short of breath and my heart wasn't thumping away. I was so pleased with myself! There's a downside to taking the anti-depressants though; I seem to be permanently hungry. It's too easy to sit and eat all the wrong foods; I must be very careful not to put on too much weight.

I've just logged in to see there's an email from Liam.

Darling,

I've been so busy at work and had to wait until the end of the day to send you an email to say that I love you more than life itself. I'm so sorry not to be able to speak to you in the mornings now, but I know Patty would make a point of being around if we did.

I think Patty might have been reading our emails while I've been at work. I've now put a password on the computer so that she can't access them anymore, but things are quite bad at home at the moment. She's accusing me of not loving her. All I can say to you is that I did love her once, but I love you more. It's not something I have any control over. I haven't said anything to her of my feelings for you because my son is so important to me, and I feel I must stay with Patty for his sake. He needs the constant presence of his daddy who loves him, so that he can develop into a loving, caring human being.

My life is such a mess. I need you like I need to breathe.

L. xxxx'

My arms ached to reach out across the miles and hold him. He was doing right by his son in being there for him, but if his partner was convinced he loved another woman then there was the possibility she could leave and take his son away from him. I didn't want to be the cause of him losing his son, so I decided not to answer any more of his emails. Amy could still speak to him at weekends, but I thought it might be best if I kept out of the way.

CHAPTER 21 - LIAM

HE LOGGED IN and looked forward to speaking to his daughter. Amy seemed a bright little thing; she was enjoying school and doing well. He scanned his inbox, but there were no emails from Beth. He sighed as he checked again; why was she not answering his messages?

"How long will you be? I thought we were going to take Toby out to the park?" Patty sounded petulant and moody.

"We will, but it's my time to speak with Amy."

"We'll be waiting for you."

He dialled Beth's number and heard the phone ring at the other end.

"Hello Liam!" Amy's girlish voice made him smile. He looked at her photo next to Toby's; she looked so uncannily like her mother. He took an inrush of breath at the sight.

"Hey Amy! I've missed you! How has school been this week?"

He couldn't take his eyes from her face in the photo. His own daughter, and she was half-grown already. He switched on the speaker and her voice filled the room.

"Okay, thanks. I came top in the maths test on Friday. I even beat Penny Green, and nobody ever usually beats her. She's not speaking to me now."

"Well done. You're a clever girl. Don't you worry your head about Penny Green; she has to learn to meet with triumph and disaster and treat those two imposters just the same. That last bit is part of a very famous poem by Rudyard Kipling."

"Miss Everett read us that one the other day. I remember it's called 'If'."

"I recall when I was a boy the whole class had detention and we couldn't go home unless we could recite it out loud from memory. I still remember the whole poem to this day."

"Wow. We have to write lines if we're naughty, but I'm not naughty though." Amy swivelled round on the office chair as she spoke.

"What are you reading now Amy?" Liam smiled and wished he could give his daughter a hug.

"George's Marvellous Medicine. It's funny, but Miss Everett wants me to start reading a book by somebody called William Shakespeare, but it's boring and I can't understand it."

"You will as you get older. Maybe Miss Everett's asking too much of you at the moment."

"Mummy says there's more books with stories about Philip, Jack, Lucy-Ann and Dinah."

"I'm going to order you the whole series on the Internet and send them to you."

"Wow! Thanks Liam, and guess what?"

"What?"

"I got in the bath last night and I didn't drown!"

"That's wonderful sweetheart. I'm very proud of you!"

"Liam. Actually, would you mind if I do call you Daddy?"

He swallowed a lump in his throat.

"No, sweetheart. I wouldn't mind at all."

He could hear Patty's voice calling from the kitchen.

"I've got Toby ready to go out now!"

"Yes ok, darling. I'll be there in a minute!" He felt a wave of irritation at the sound of her voice.

"Is Mummy there, Amy?"

"Not in the room. She's in the kitchen with Granny getting tea."

"Can you tell her I'd like to speak to her please?"

"Okay." Amy gave a final swivel on the chair and jumped off. After a few moments she returned, and Liam's heart gave an extra beat.

"Amy, could you find that book you have about Philip and Jack and the others and let me know who wrote it please? I just want to make sure I get the author right?"

"Okay!" Amy ran off happily to find her book, and Liam took advantage of the few minutes he had alone with Beth.

"Hello darling. I've missed you so much! Why haven't you answered my emails?"

"Liam, I don't think it's right we should be doing this."

"Do you love me?"

"Of course I do. I always have."

"Then it's right. I can't function without speaking to you."

"What about Patty?"

"Don't you worry about Patty."

"But I do. I don't want to be the one that breaks up your family."

"Too late! You already have!"

A voice behind him startled Liam. He had been too wrapped up in looking at Beth to notice anyone coming into the office. He turned around and saw Patty's flame-red hair and matching furious face. She was holding Toby who was desperate to escape her vice-like grip. He struggled and cried and her eyes smouldered with hate as they looked over his head towards the screen. Liam's heart sank.

"Patty, this is my time with Amy. Please can you give us a minute?"

"I can hear that Amy isn't even in the room! I knew you were talking to her!"

At that moment he heard Amy come back. He could hear Beth's voice in the background coming through the speaker, trying to divert their daughter away from the seriousness of the situation.

"Amy; I think Granny needs a hand with tea."

"Oh but I need to speak to Daddy about my book!" Amy's voice had taken on a whining tone.

"I'll show it to Daddy don't worry. Come back when you've helped Granny."

"We were ok until you appeared! Me, Liam, and Toby. We were a happy family. Now Liam's sending you love letters and God knows what else! Mind your own fucking business and keep out of our lives!"

Patty was incandescent with rage. Toby screamed as loudly as he could manage.

"Granny says she doesn't need any more help!"

Liam could hear that Amy had reappeared and was probably standing there next to Beth. Shocked, torn, and under pressure he did the only thing he could think of; he clicked the receiver down and ended the call.

"I'm going with Toby to Mom's! You bastard! You can't function without seeing her? Well fuck off back to England then!"

The office door slammed, and then the front door banged with a force to wake up the dead. Liam heard Patty start the car and then speed off down the road. He put his head in his hands and cried.

CHAPTER 22 - LIAM

HE WAS NOT sure how long he'd sat there, too dazed and stupefied to move. He listened to the sound of emails arriving but could no more bring himself to answer them than fly to the moon.

Surely Patty would be back with Toby soon? Surely she hadn't left him for good? The thought that he might never see his little son again was too awful to contemplate. He would have to apologise. He'd been so wrapped up in thinking about Beth that he'd completely forgotten all about Patty's feelings; of course she would feel threatened by another woman appearing on the scene. He mentally kicked himself for being an absolute twat.

He reached over towards the telephone and scrolled down the menu looking for the number of the woman he could never quite manage to impress.

"Hi Cathy; Liam here. Can I speak to Patty please?"

There was an audible sigh at the other end.

"I'll tell her you're on the line. Hold on."

It seemed like an eternity but in reality it was probably only a minute or so before he heard the receiver being picked up again.

"What do you want?" Patty's voice was cold and completely without emotion.

"I want you and Toby to come back home. I'm so sorry for what happened earlier. It won't happen again."

"That's because you'll speak to her in secret or when I'm not there."

"No. I'll only speak to Amy from now on. That's how it's going to be."

"Pull the other one; it's got bells on."

"No, I mean it. I'm missing you both already."

"I'm not coming home tonight. Toby's settled and asleep now. I'm not going to be second best Liam. You can't do that to me. You have to choose; her or me."

"You're not second best. Please come home."

"No way. You have a think about who you want to be with."

There was a click at the other end as the receiver was lowered. Liam sighed; he looked towards the computer screen and saw he had three emails, all from Beth:

Dear Liam,

I'm terribly sorry about what happened just now. I should never have come into the room when Amy called. Can you forgive me?

Beth x'

He clicked on the next message:

'Dearest Liam,

Are things ok with you and Patty? Please can you email me back and let me know what's happening.

Love Beth x'

By the time he'd read the third email he knew his relationship with Patty was doomed.

'My dearest Liam,

I realise that possibly I've come between you and Patty and that you don't wish to contact me. I'm so sorry. I never wanted to cause any trouble. I think it best that we don't contact or see each other again. Of course you can talk to Amy at the weekends and see her in the school holidays, but that's as far as it goes and I will not be in the room when you telephone her. Please show this email to Patty so that she knows how I feel.

Again please accept my apologies for causing any distress to you and Patty.

Beth x'

He felt fresh tears forming at the thought of never being able to see Beth again or hear her voice. He picked up the phone and tried to call her, but the tone sounded as though she had taken the receiver off the hook. He wiped his eyes with the back of his hand and began to type a message. If both relationships were doomed but he now had the chance to salvage one of them, he somehow knew which one it was going to be.

My own darling Beth,

I've tried to call you on the phone, but I keep getting the engaged tone.

There is no way you have caused any trouble. I loved you for years before Patty ever appeared on the scene, and I cannot switch off my emotions. Now that I know you're alive I cannot live with the knowledge that I'll never see your face again or be able to speak to you. If I had known we would meet again in the future I would never have looked for anybody else. Patty is never going to be able to fill the enormous gap that you left in my heart; she has given me a beautiful son and I will always stay fond of her, but I cannot help my feelings towards you. I will have to tell Patty that I love you more.

Do you still love me? How would you feel about bringing the children over to Toronto for a couple of weeks' vacation at Easter? Would you be ok with the travelling (you would probably feel fine on the Citalopram by then)? I'll pay your fares. We can get to know each other all over again, and I can get to know my daughter better. I could meet you at the airport and we could stay in my family's cottage near Kincardine, on the shores of Lake Huron. The weather probably won't be too good, but there's a lovely wood burner inside the cottage and we'll be cosy and warm. We can drive into Kincardine for supplies, and there's a weekly market there that you'll like.

If you're agreeable and want to be with me again I'll take the next couple of months to find some suitable accommodation for myself so that Patty and Toby can have the house. I'll try and smooth it over with Patty so that I can at least keep in touch with Toby. When I have a new place and I'm on my own I'll call you and we'll be able to talk again and make future plans. I realize now that I needed to make a choice, and I have just done so. I love my son desperately but I cannot live without you in my life. Please come back to me. I love you. I have always loved you. I will never stop loving you.

Please let me know how you feel. I want you back in my life.

All my love forever, Liam xxxx'

With a heavy heart he turned off the computer and ran a hand through his hair. He had no idea how Beth would reply, if indeed she was going to reply at all. Above the monitor was a photo he'd taken of Patty and Toby, happy and smiling after a picnic on the beach the previous summer. Their world would soon be turned upside down, and Liam knew that as his son grew older he might never want to make contact again. At that precise moment he hated himself for what he might have to do to Toby because he couldn't love Patty enough.

He tossed and turned that night; once again sleep eluded him. At 3am he went downstairs and switched on the computer, and the message he'd been waiting for popped up on the screen.

Darling Liam,

I love you. I'll wait forever for your call.

All my love,
Beth
Xxxxxxxxxxxxxxxxxxxxxxxx'

He went back to bed and slept like a baby.

The alarm's shrill sound cut into his dream. He'd been at the cottage, standing with his arms around Beth on the decking, and looking out at the sunset over the lake. Eyes closed, he reached an arm over to the other side of the bed, but the feeling of completeness soon faded when his hand touched nothing but a cold sheet.

Wide awake and with a feeling of impending doom, he quickly showered and dressed, ate a bowl of cereal and caught the tram to his morning clinical practice downtown. On returning he could see their car in the driveway, signalling that Patty was home.

As he turned the key in the lock his heart gave a lurch at the sight of his son running down the passageway to greet him.

"Daddy! Daddy!"

Toby raised his arms and Liam gathered him up, pressing his face into the warm sweet-smelling neck.

"Hi little fella! Daddy's so pleased to see you!" He kissed Toby, enjoying the feel of the baby's head upon his shoulder.

"He's due for his afternoon nap now." Patty came out into the hallway and unsmiling, took the baby and went upstairs.

Pouring some coffee from the percolator while Toby was settling in his cot, Liam wondered how many more times he would perform such an everyday task in the kitchen that he'd lovingly designed himself. He'd never really thought about it before, but then again he'd never been on the verge of moving out.

Uncertain as to whether it was the shot of caffeine or the sound of Patty's footsteps on the stairs making his heart beat faster, he turned around as she came into the room.

"Well? Have you made your mind up then?"

Liam thought she looked more beautiful than ever. She'd obviously taken time and trouble with her makeup, and the effect was stunning. However, his heart belonged to one person, and one person only.

"I'm so sorry Patty. I lost her for ten years and I just can't lose her a second time. She offered to never contact me again so that you and I could be together, but I just can't do it. Forgive me. I'm such a bastard." He moved forward to take her in his arms, but she backed away."

"Don't come anywhere near me! This is it; we're finished, you and me. You'll never see Toby again!" She began to cry at the hopelessness of the situation.

"You can have this house. I'll pay the mortgage and give you a monthly allowance, but I'm entitled to see my son." He started to panic at the implication of her words.

"Not if I have anything to do with it! And I wouldn't live in this house if you paid me all the money in the world!"

"Please Patty, be reasonable! I'll go through the courts if I have to, but I want access to Toby."

"Now I know why you never asked me to marry you! You were waiting for her!" She spat out the words with a venom he never knew existed.

He sighed and sat down at the table, exhausted and emotionally drained.

"I thought she was dead; that's why I never bothered telling you. It was all over and in the past, but then she reappears out of the blue. I just can't ignore her as if she still doesn't exist. And then there's Amy whom I need to get to know. I'm so sorry. I have to be with Beth."

"Then Toby and I are in your way. I'll be moving back with Mom until I find another place."

Calmer now after her outburst, she looked at him, dried her tears, and then walked out of the kitchen to begin organising a new life in which he was certain he would be playing no part.

CHAPTER 23

THE LANDING GEAR hit the tarmac of Pearson International airport and the passengers' applause was enough to wake Joss from his sleep.

"Are we there now?" Amy looked excitedly out of the cabin window as the plane came to a halt.

"Yes. Daddy will be waiting for us when we've collected our suitcases." The thought of seeing Liam's face in the Arrivals hall had kept Beth going throughout the ordeal of being cooped up in her seat with two children for the duration of the seven hour flight. She hoped he wouldn't notice the few extra pounds she'd gained on the Citalopram.

"Come on. Don't forget your book."

She relished the chance to stand up and retrieve her bag from the overhead luggage compartment. Putting the strap over her shoulder she picked up Joss from the bassinette and followed Amy out of the aeroplane and into the terminal building, glad of the cool fresh afternoon air on her face.

"Where do we go now, Mummy?"

"We have to go to the baggage collection point. Look at the TV screen and it'll show us what number carousel to go to."

"What's a carousel?"

"You'll see in a minute." She smiled at her daughter's curiosity that at present knew no bounds.

Thankfully the pushchair was one of the first items to come through. Strapping her son in securely and giving instructions to Amy to stay with the baby, Beth found a trolley and waited by the carousel for the rest of the baggage. The first sight of his smiling daughter pushing Joss, and of Beth following wearily behind with the trolley full of suitcases would stay with him for a long time and confirm to him that he'd made the right decision.

"There's Daddy!"

Amy's mothering skills took a slight downward turn as she ran towards her father on the other side of the barrier.

"Don't forget Joss!"

Liam pointed at the sleeping baby. Amy laughed and ran back to retrieve her brother.

"It's so good to see you all!"

He kissed them one by one. Beth felt familiar arms around her and had a sense of coming home.

"I've waited so long for this moment!" She buried her head in his chest and let the tears fall.

"Why are you crying, Mummy?" Amy rocked the baby back and forth and looked at her parents in surprise.

"Because I'm happy. Daddy and I have looked forward to this holiday for a long time."

"Will I see the big waterfall that you told me about?"

"We're going to relax in a cottage on the beach for a week, and then we'll drive to Niagara for the second week."

Beth wiped her eyes and reluctantly pulled herself away from Liam's chest.

"Let's get going, it's a bit of a drive to Kincardine, but we'll stop in Elmira for dinner on the way." Liam took the trolley and headed out towards the short term car parks.

The car was spacious, with plenty of room for the pushchair. Beth saw the baby car seat and had a pang of guilt when she thought how Liam must have bought the car with his own son in mind.

"It's a people carrier. There's a lot of these cars over here. The middle seats fold down if you want some extra space."

"Wow! There's so much room in the back!" Amy looked around appreciatively. "Wait until I tell Penny Green at school!"

"I thought she wasn't speaking to you?" Liam smiled at Amy.

"She is now. We're best friends."

"That's good news."

As the car turned onto the A401 West, Beth sat behind Liam with the children and marvelled at the wide freeway, complete with an express lane in the middle for drivers that had no need to exit for a long time and priority lanes for people carrying more than one passenger.

"The roads in England seem tiny by comparison." Her head swivelled from left to right.

"We do things on a big scale on the other side of the pond. Ok at the back, Amy?"

"Joss is asleep, and I'm reading one of the books you sent me. They're great. Thanks Liam –er…Daddy."

Beth awoke as the car approached Elmira and Joss stirred, hunger pangs gnawing.

"Sorry Liam, I didn't mean to nod off." She gave Joss some water and Amy fidgeted in her seat.

"Don't worry about it. I've never worked out why air travel is so tiring. You just sit in the seat doing nothing, but you're exhausted at the end of the flight."

"I need a wee, Mummy."

"We're stopping for dinner now, so there'll be washrooms in the restaurant." Liam turned his head towards his daughter as he pulled up in the car park.

"I don't need a wash, I need a wee." "A washroom is a Canadian toilet." "Oh."

"Amy, you'll find the ladies serving here are dressed in an old-fashioned way. They're all Mennonites, and they belong to a big group of religious people who prefer not to use the modern labour-saving devices. They still dress as people did over 100 years ago, and they drive a horse and buggy instead of a car. They've made all the food in this restaurant themselves, and you'll find it's delicious." You'll also see all the roads around here for miles have little gravel paths down either side especially for the Mennonite horse and carriages."

"Wow. Why would people not want to buy a car? Cars are so much faster than a horse and buggy!" Amy looked out of the car window to see if any Mennonite families were passing by.

"It's just their way. Many of them are farmers and they use all the old farming skills instead of ploughs and combine harvesters."

"That's so interesting, but don't the young people rebel?"

Beth wondered if the teenagers could resist the lure of the mobile phone, TV and computer.

"They are allowed to go out into the big wide world to see if they prefer it, but surprisingly most of them return to the old way of life after a while."

Beth unstrapped Joss and gathered a bottle of milk from the cool bag.

"I hope we're not too far away now, this is the last but one bottle."

"It's roughly about another two hours. Mom lives in Kincardine, and she's filled up the fridge for us at the cottage. There's loads of baby bits there because other members of the family bring little ones. You'll meet Mom tomorrow. Her parents bought the cottage when they were first married. It's a bit of a family heirloom now."

"I can't wait. Thanks so much for inviting us. I actually went out to Cley to visit your dad last month with the children. He loved them. He seemed so pleased to see me." Beth followed Liam in to the restaurant.

"I know. He told me on the phone. He's always liked you. He's got good taste."

He kissed her and announced their arrival to the receptionist behind the front desk.

"Table for three and a high chair please."

"Of course. Please come this way."

They were shown to an empty table in amongst several others that were already full of diners. Against the walls were large buffet tables groaning with every kind of food imaginable. Smiling Mennonite ladies weaved to and fro in amongst the tables as they served drinks.

"I keep thinking I'm back in the 1880's!" Beth whispered.

"Mummy I need a wee!"

"Liam, can you start Joss with his bottle please? I'll show Amy where the toilets are."

"They're washrooms, don't forget." Liam chuckled

"Oh yes. It does sound better though doesn't it?" Beth laughed as she and Amy stood up.

Liam cuddled the baby close and gazed at him as he contentedly sucked at the bottle. He suddenly wondered what Toby was doing, and if he was missing his daddy.

CHAPTER 24 - BETH

"LIAM, THAT WAS just the most gorgeous meal I've ever eaten!" Beth leaned back in the chair, replete.

"It's pretty wonderful food, eh? I always stop here on the way to see Mom. You know everything's fresh and homemade. I'll get the check and then we can be on our way again."

"I'll just change the baby's nappy first." Beth started to make her way back to the washroom.

"It's not a nappy, it's a diaper."

"Or is it diaper, eh?"

"Touché!"

Both children were asleep within a short time of the car pulling out onto the road. Beth climbed into the front seat and enjoyed sitting next to Liam in the gathering darkness and feeling comfortable enough not to have to make any conversation. Every now and then a Mennonite horse and buggy would pass by on the side of the road; the family inside staring straight ahead and unsmiling in their Victorian apparel.

"What a way to live! It doesn't seem to fit in with to-day's fast pace though." Beth found that she was becoming fascinated by the Mennonite way of life.

"It's what they know; they're born to it. Some of them are quite wealthy. Have a look at their houses that you can see spread out. The majority of them don't even have any electricity."

"Good God."

The land had flattened out, and on either side Beth could see low buildings and miles of open farmland. She felt happy to be at one with the earth and the sky, and to be able to sneak little glances at Liam's profile as he drove into the night.

"Happy?" Liam turned to her, conscious of her eyes watching him as they passed by the outskirts of Kincardine.

"I'm in heaven, I swear. I don't know if it's being with you, being out of that awful prison, or being on the Citalopram though!"

"Hopefully it's being with me that's doing it, eh?" A small smile played about his lips as he spoke.

"You bet!" She relaxed in her seat as they drove along the coast road.

"We'll be there in five. Don't go back to sleep."

"Oh, I can see the sea! Amy will be delighted."

"It's Lake Huron, not the sea. The water isn't salty."

"Wow. I can't wait to see it in the daylight."

"The cottage backs onto the beach. You'll see it tomorrow."

He swung the steering wheel to the right, turned up a narrow track, and brought the car to a halt in front of a 1930's white clapboard cottage surrounded by tall trees and hedges. Beth could see a light shining behind the blue front door.

"Mom's been and gone by now. It's all ready for us."

"It's wonderful. I love the shutters on the windows."

"The cottage is usually closed up this early in the year, but Mom would have lit the log burner so it'll be nice and warm inside."

Beth eased Joss from his car seat and Liam held Amy. Together they carried the sleeping children up the few wooden steps and into the kitchen.

"The front door wasn't locked." Beth whispered and looked around.

"Nobody locks their doors around here. There's no need to." Liam placed Amy carefully on one of the bunk beds and took off her socks and shoes.

"Don't wake her up, I'll sort through the cases tomorrow and find her pyjamas." Beth covered her daughter up, noticing the attractive bedspread.

"Mom made the quilt when I was born. Every stitch was sewn with love." Liam whispered and smiled.

"I can't wait to meet her again." Beth smiled back as she placed the baby in his cot. "I need to make up some bottles for Joss now in case he wakes up in the night."

"Everything you'll need will be in the kitchen. Mom knows about these things."

Beth made her way back to the kitchen, approving of the welcoming feel of the cottage. Scores of old family photographs hung upon the walls of the main living area, which had obviously been set up to accommodate many branches of the family all at the same time. Liam as a moody toddler stared out at her from the wall adjacent to the back door which led out to the sun deck. Comfortable sofas and armchairs surrounded a low central table. The log burner gave out a pleasing heat, and children's toys were scattered about in large baskets. A bookshelf of well-thumbed novels stood in one corner behind the TV.

"Oh Liam it's such a lovely cottage. I'm going to love it here."

"And I love you, baby." He put his arms around her and laid his cheek against the top of her warm head.

"Love you too. I'll make up the bottles and then have a nice hot bath."

"Ah. No bath I'm afraid; only a shower. We Canadians like showers."

"Ok. A nice hot shower then!" She kissed him and put the kettle on to boil.

Refreshed and glowing and wrapped in a towel, Beth rooted around in the suitcase for her night clothes. She smiled as she heard Liam singing in the shower. She could hardly be-lieve that only a few months had passed since being freed from Evans' grip.

By the time Liam had come out of the shower Beth had made herself comfortable on the sofa in front of the log burner. Her eyes felt heavy.

"Room for another one on there?" He sat down by her side wearing a clean t-shirt and jogging trousers, and smelling of a mixture of shower gel and toothpaste.

"Absolutely. I think I'm in heaven, but I don't remem-ber dying." She smiled as she cuddled up to him.

"And you haven't. You've got a lot of living to do first." He kissed her lips and she buried her head in his shoulder.

"Liam, I think I ought to get something out in the open straight away. I don't know if I'm ready for a physical relationship again yet. I hope you understand." She breathed a sigh of relief at getting the worry off her chest.

"Of course. You've been through a lot. If you want to sleep alone there are plenty of beds here. I totally understand." He held her tighter and she relaxed in his arms.

"I'm so sorry.   It's just that............."   She broke off, unable to go on any further.

"I know. I have a pretty good idea of what he did to you. If I ever hear that he's got out of jail he'd better keep looking over his shoulder. We'll just take it one day at a time."

"I'm so sorry."

"Don't be. I don't want to hear another word about it. Just keep cuddling me."

"I can do that. I don't want to sleep alone though like I have to do at Mum and Dad's; I'm so used to Amy in the bed with me. Is it fair to ask you?"

"Well, there's nobody else about and Amy's asleep, so I guess it'll have to be me then." They snuggled nearer, enjoying the closeness.

"We used to sleep naked. Do you remember?" She sighed and listened to the clock ticking on the wall.

"How could I forget? We used to lay together like two spoons." He tried unsuccessfully to block the memory."

"I can't do it again just yet."

"Will you behave yourself? I told you, I don't want to hear another word."

She lifted her head and kissed his neck.

"Can you stroke my hair like you used to?" She closed her eyes and smelt the warmth of him.

"Sure can. I'm good at stroking, but there's not much hair to play with these days." He took a small piece of the blonde hair between his fingers and twirled it around.

"I couldn't bear it any longer. The way he looked at it and touched it; I used to cringe inside. If he'd ever given me a knife or a pair of scissors I would have cut it off myself."

"I'll never do anything to you that you don't want me to." He kissed her hair and felt tears forming in his eyes. He blinked them away.

"Will I ever be able to get over this?" She looked up at him and his heart gave a lurch.

"With time, darling. I'll help as much as I can. I'll be your counsellor. Soon the good times will outweigh the bad."

She gazed into the fire.

"What about your little boy? Will Patty let you see him?"

"She wouldn't at first, but then she told me he kept ask-ing for his daddy and she's relented. I've only seen him a few times in the last couple of months though, but she's thawing out a bit now I think. It'll get better in the long run."

"I'm so glad. He'll need his daddy as he grows up. Where are they living now?"

"With her mother. I'm as good as dead though as far as Cathy's concerned. I've given Patty money for a new place."

"Of course. So you've kept the old place in Toronto?"

"Yes. It's turned into a bachelor pad now. It needs a woman's touch again."

"Will I see it before I go back?"

"Sure. It's not too far from the airport."

He ruffled her hair.

"Come on; time for bed. I want to be your spoon."

With Liam's warmth against her back, she knew no more until daybreak.

CHAPTER 25 - BETH

THE SOUND OF a baby's cries broke through her dreamless sleep.

"Mummy! Where are you? Joss is hungry!"

Amy's worried voice at finding herself in unfamiliar surroundings brought Beth suddenly back to reality. She felt Liam's arm tighten around her waist as she began to climb out of bed.

"Let's stay here all day." He yawned and chuckled.

"Oh yes, that'll work well with our two little people." She gently removed his arm, swung her legs over the side of the bed, and rooted around for her slippers.

"Just kidding. Let's get up and at 'em!"

"I'm in here darling!" She smiled as the bedroom door flew open and Amy appeared.

"I looked out of the window, and all I can see is water! Is that the sea like Philip and Jack sailed on in Bill Smugs' boat?"

"It's Lake Huron, Amy. When we've had breakfast we'll wrap up warmly and go down onto the beach. You won't want to swim in it though, it's very cold at this time of the year." Liam wrapped a dressing gown around him and followed Amy and Beth out to the kitchen.

"I can't swim yet anyway. Mummy, can I pick Joss up out of his cot?"

"Yes of course. I'll warm up his bottle."

She placed a bottle of formula milk into the microwave. Liam came up behind her and put his arms around her waist.

"Love you so much, honey. I'm so glad you're here." He kissed the top of her head.

"Me too. It's a dream come true. I used to think about you every day and wonder what you were doing."

"Mummy, Joss has done a poo!" Amy entered the kitchen, wrinkled her nose, and handed the baby to her mother.

"Babies do tend to do that Amy. Tell you what; I'll change his diaper and Mommy will fix you some cereal, eh?" Liam laughed as Beth handed Joss to him.

"Can I sleep in your bed tonight like I used to in the house with no windows?" Amy carefully poured cereal into a bowl.

"Well, Daddy sleeps with me now darling. You have your own bed here like you do at Nanny and Grandpa's house."

"Why does Daddy sleep in your bed and I can't?"

"You slept in my bed because there was nowhere else for you to sleep and there was no room to put another bed down. Children usually sleep in their own bedrooms in houses that have windows. This house has windows, and Nanny and Grandpa's house has windows." Beth shook the bottle of baby milk and hoped she'd given a good enough explanation.

"Why doesn't Daddy have his own bedroom here?" Amy was not going to be put off so easily.

"Daddy is not a child. You and Joss have your own rooms and Daddy and I share now. It's what grown-ups do." Beth gave a sigh of irritation as she waited for the next question.

"So can I sleep in your bed when I'm grown up then?"

Beth smiled at the childlike logic and gave in.

"Yes; when you're grown up, but only if you still want to."

She sat down in the peace and quiet of the main living area and fed her son with the sound of the lake lapping against the shore in the background. She looked down at the baby, and two soulful brown eyes stared back. What wisps of hair he did have on his head were dark.

He had his father's eyes. She would never forget those eyes for as long as she lived.

She turned to look out towards the lake, and tried to ignore the tears that were blurring her vision.

Joss was her saviour. He'd released her from a hell on earth. Why was she suddenly thinking about Evans? She had Liam back now. All was well.

"Some coffee here for you." Liam placed a steaming cup on the table in front of her.

"Thanks. I'm nearly done now."

"Amy's getting dressed. She wants to go down on the beach."

"Yes; give me another half an hour and I'm there."

Warmly dressed against the March elements and carefully holding the baby, she followed Liam and Amy out of the back door, across the decking, and down a wooden flight of stairs. Standing on the sand close to Liam with the chilly wind on her face, she watched her daughter run happily along the vast expanse of empty beach.

"This is a dream come true for her, and for me. You've no idea." She cuddled her son closer, pulling a blanket in around him.

"It's quite a bit warmer in the summer, but there'll be more people around."

"I'll bring a bikini next time then."

"I'll look forward to that." He kissed her and waved to Amy. "Mom and Harry will be here soon. They're probably on their way now."

With some reluctance she called Amy and went back upstairs to await the arrival of the mother-in-law she was cheated out of. Within a short time the sound of a car's engine could be heard on the track outside. As she stood with Liam and Amy in the doorway of the cottage, a well-dressed woman in her fifties climbed excitedly out of the car and ran quickly up the steps.

"Beth, it's so good to see you again!" Constance Ayres kissed the woman whom her son obviously adored, and whom she wished could have become her daughter in law.

"Connie! We meet again at last! This is your grand-daughter Amy."

"Hello." Amy shyly came forward to meet her grand-mother.

"My, my! What a pretty child! She has the look of Liam about her."

"Yes I know. The older she gets the more she's looking just like him."

Beth turned her gaze to a tall, elegant, quiet middle-aged man keeping himself in the background as Connie made the introductions.

"Beth, this is Harry. We've been married a few years now."

"Hi, Beth! Pleased to meet you!" Harry kissed her and solemnly shook Amy's hand. "That's a fine little brother you have there, Amy!"

"He's called Joss, after Philip's uncle."

"Who's Philip?"

"He's in my old book, but I don't read it now. I used to read it when I slept with Mummy in the house with no windows. Daddy sleeps with Mummy now because they're grown-ups, and I have a new book that Daddy bought me."

"I see." Harry looked slightly puzzled.

"Shall we go into Kincardine? The market's on this morning." Connie saw the look of embarrassment briefly fall across her son's face, and decided to change the subject.

"Sure. I'll just put a clean nappy on Joss and then we'll be ready." Beth reminded herself to have a little word with her daughter in private regarding their sleeping arrangements.

"Lunch out; our treat!" Connie took Amy's hand. "Come and see the sea Granny!" Amy pulled her grandmother towards the back window.

"It's a lake, darling. It eventually drains into the sea, but it's a lake." Connie laughed at Amy's exuberance.

"Daddy says we can swim in it in the summer. I'm learning to swim at school, but have to put armbands on."

"Daddy could swim by the time he was five years old." Constance then mentally kicked herself for running her mouth before putting her brain into gear.

"We only had a sink in the house with no windows."

"Of course. You'll soon learn. Don't worry."

"Ready to go?" Liam popped his head around the bedroom door.

"Yep. One clean bum for five minutes."

"Butt. It's a butt, or an ass." He loved to make her laugh. The dimples were still there on her cheeks when her mouth turned up at the corners.

"I'll smack your butt if you don't shut up."

"Promises....promises!" He took the baby from her and watched as she put on her coat. "You look beautiful. I can't take my eyes off you."

"You're not so bad yourself. Come on, they're waiting for us."

She took his hand and kissed his lips. He moved his free hand around her waist and touched the tip of her tongue with his own.

"I can't live without you." He buried his face in her hair and sighed.

"Mummy! Daddy! We're ready!" Amy threw open the bedroom door.

"You'll have to learn to knock, Amy." Liam hoped his jacket covered his growing erection.

"Why?"

"Well, grown-ups might not be ready even though children are." He heard Beth stifle a giggle as she let go of his hand.

"Granny's going to take us out to lunch to a restaurant overlooking the harbour. She says there's a light house and sometimes there's a piper with a bag walking around it."

Liam laughed out loud.

"Not this morning there isn't. Amy, you're a princess!"

"I'm not! I don't want to be a princess!" She ran out of the room suddenly and into the waiting car.

"Did I say something wrong?" He looked at Beth questioningly.

"*He* always called her his princess. She hated it."

"Oh God, sorry; I had no idea."

"It's ok; she's doing really well, but every now and then something will remind her of him. You weren't to know."

"I'll be extra careful from now on."

CHAPTER 26 - BETH

"I THINK SHE'S forgiven me. When I read her a story to-night she gave me a hug."

"You're on a winner then. If you're out of favour she'll soon let you know about it."

They cuddled together on the sofa, clean after a shower and feeling warm and cosy.

"Your mum's great. I remember seeing her years ago when she came over to visit your dad in Cley. She still looks the same."

"Harry's keeping her young. He's about five years her junior."

"She got herself a toy-boy? Good for her!" Beth snuggled into Liam's shoulder, smelling his warmth and feeling safe in his arms.

"Can I be your toy-boy?" He stroked her hair and then rested his arm around her shoulders.

"I think it's the other way around. You're older than me, but I don't think the six month age gap is going to make much of a difference."

"When is Amy's birthday?" He suddenly realised he had no idea of the date of his own daughter's birth.

"Your guess is as good as mine. Dad registered her birth and I told him to use Christmas Day 1987, as that was probably my due date. We can always have a double celebration then at Christmas, and it's made Amy feel special to have a Christmas birthday."

He reached down to brush his lips against her forehead. She raised her head and found his lips with her own. Their tongues intermingled and she was aware of a throbbing sensation deep in her groin that she hadn't felt for a very long time.

"I love you so much." He thought his body would burst with the frustration of wanting to touch her.

"Oh Liam, I don't want to be anywhere else except right here with you at this moment."

"Come to bed. Let me hold you in my arms. You're my world; my everything. I can't even think straight anymore."

She took his hand and led him to the bedroom. She thanked her lucky stars she had listened to her mother's advice and had recommenced taking the contraceptive pill. She never thought she would ever want to have sex again. She thought back to the last time they had made love. So much had changed; she would never be the same person again, but right at that moment she was as near as she could get to the 26 year old carefree and trusting young woman that she used to be.

She was shaking as she let her nightclothes fall to the floor.

"My God, Beth. You're so beautiful. I love you so much!" Naked, he came over to her and lifted her up in his arms. "Will you marry me? I'll never let you go again."

She had waited a lifetime to hear those words. Before she lost herself in his kiss she managed to stumble out the few words he had been waiting to hear:

"Yes. I'll marry you. You're the only man I've ever truly loved."

She gave herself to him willingly and with a strange delight that was both new but somehow familiar, and if the world had stopped outside they would have both been unaware. Their pent up emotion was released in a shuddering wave of mutual pleasure as their bodies found their old rhythm and rocked in complete harmony as though time had stood still. She knew that if she closed her eyes and tried hard enough she could even imagine they were back in the old double room they had shared at the hospital; before Amy, before Joss, and before Edwin.

"Never leave me again. I don't want to live if you're not with me." He lay on her body, spent and sated.

"I'll never leave you, darling." She put her arms around his neck and let the tears fall from her eyes, feeling the weight of his body and the love for her in his heart.

"Together we're strong. We'll face anything." He worried momentarily that he might be too heavy, and so rolled onto his side and pulled her towards him.

They lay together, enjoying the easy familiarity they had once shared.

"Where do you want us to get married? Do you want to live here or in the UK?" Beth propped herself up on one elbow, eager to receive Liam's reply.

"I don't care. On the moon if you like. As long as I can keep in touch with Toby I'll live where you want. I can set up a clinic anywhere. I have dual nationality, so it'll probably be easier if we live in the UK in that respect." At that precise moment he felt he could have inhabited a cardboard box.

"I was hoping you'd say that. Amy loves her school and I don't want to uproot her."

"Fine by me. It'll take me a while to close down the clinic here and get set up again in the UK, but when I come to the UK it'll be for good. We'll come back to Toronto when we can to see Toby, and Mom will obviously let us use the cottage as often as possible."

"It all sounds so easy in theory."

"When you fly home I won't be too far behind you. Before the summer's out we'll be married, I promise." He kissed her passionately and felt himself becoming hard again.

She enjoyed the sight of his eyes devouring her body. She lay back wantonly against the pillow, reaching back with her arms above her head. She parted her legs as he lay on her again, and wrapped them around his back. They made love slowly for a second time; the urgency was gone. Taking great care, they delighted in exploring each other's bodies until the owls could be heard hooting in the trees outside.

"Love you, Dr Darrah." Beth could safely say that she had never felt as cherished as she did right at that moment.

"Love you too, my darling."

They fell asleep locked in each other's arms.

CHAPTER 27 - BETH

"THIS IS THE touristy bit. You'll see the real thing when we cross over the road and turn right."

Beth felt overcome with the sights and sounds of Clifton Hill. Checking that Joss was still happy in his baby carrier on Liam's back, she held on tightly to Amy's hand as they weaved in and out through crowds of excited holidaymakers. The cacophony from the amusement arcades on either side of them spilled out into the street.

"Mummy, can we go in?"

Amy's gaze was drawn to a particularly noisome arcade, with a child posing for a photo outside it who was sitting astride a large Harley Davidson motorbike clamped to a stand.

"No, not now. On the way back to the hotel perhaps." Beth wasn't sure she could stand the noise even for one moment.

"We'll see the waterfall quite soon, Amy." Liam still remembered his first view of the Horseshoe Falls when he had been not much older than Joss. As far as he was concerned its magic never really went away.

Crossing over the main road at the bottom of the hill, Amy was the first to speak.

"There it is! That's Niagara Falls!" She jumped up and down in excitement.

"No, that's the Rainbow Falls, and to the left of it is the Rainbow Bridge. When you walk across the middle of the bridge you're in America. There's a spot right in the centre with a marker. Somewhere Mom's got a photo of me as a kid with one leg in Canada and one leg in the USA. We'll walk along a bit more and you'll see an even bigger waterfall." Liam smiled at his daughter's enthusiasm, and put an arm around Beth's shoulders.

"Okay Beth?" He smiled at the woman he adored. "Yes.

It's beautiful here. Not sure about that street we've just walked down though."

"We can go back a different way if you like, and give Clifton Hill a miss."

"Good idea!" Beth laughed and gave her little finger to Joss to grip. The baby gave her a toothless smile.

"Wow! Look, Mummy!"

The first glimpse of Niagara Falls in the distance would stay in Beth's mind forever. The sound of millions of gallons of water pounding into the Niagara River below the escarpment almost took her breath away. Seagulls flew amidst the white flume that reached up almost as high as the waterfall itself. A small boat bobbed about on the waves.

"Look at all those people on that boat! They're all wearing the same colour coats!" Amy looked in amazement at the tourists hanging over the boat's railings with their cameras.

"The boat is called The Maid of the Mist, Amy. We can go on it if you like. It takes you right up to the waterfall. People on the boat are all given those blue plastic covers to stop them becoming too wet." Liam ignored the look of concern on Beth's face.

"Oh Daddy, can we? What about Joss? Can he come?"

"Sure. Babies have smaller covers. We'll put one on him and put him back in the carrier."

"No, Liam. I don't want to go." Beth shook her head while still gazing at the mesmerising effect of the cascading water.

"You'll be quite safe. Honestly."

"Somehow I don't think so." Beth's heart began to pound at the thought of it.

"Do this, and you'll be able to do anything. Step outside of your comfort zone. You'll be so proud of yourself!"

"Come on Mummy – we've got to do it! I've got to tell Penny Green where I've been!" Amy let go of her mother's hand and went to stand by the railings overlooking the river.

Beth took another look at the blue-covered tourists down amongst the whirling waters.

"How long will I be on the boat? Amy, come away from the railings!"

"About half an hour. That's all."

"Ok, I'll do it, but I'll be as frightened as a rabbit in the headlights."

"I told you, you'll be safe, I promise." Liam kissed her and stopped any further protestations."

"Ewww! Stop all that kissing!" Amy launched herself between them.

"We can kiss, Amy, because we're going to get married. How do you like that?" Liam ruffled the top of his daughter's head.

"Really? Wow! That's awesome!"

"You sound like a Canadian already, eh?"

"Would you like to be our bridesmaid?" Beth looked at their daughter and smiled.

"What will I have to do?" Amy had a puzzled look on her face.

"Look pretty and walk behind me."

"Great! Okay!"

Wearing their blue plastic covers, they waited in line to board The Maid of the Mist. Joss slept soundly on Liam's back, but Beth started to have second thoughts when they began shuffling onto the boat. She sat on a bench and watched Liam and Amy mingling with the tourists standing against the handrail.

"Here we go!" Liam glanced back and gave a thumbs up to Beth. "Come here, I've saved you a place!"

Reluctantly she came and stood in front of him. He placed his arms around her waist and kissed the top of her head.

"You'll love this. Feel the power of the water. A young boy was washed over the waterfall years ago and survived. Did you know that?"

"Good God. His poor parents. Amy, hold on to the rail!"

"I'm okay Mummy! When I was in the house with no windows I thought about going on a boat ride, and now I am!" Beth saw her child's face shining with joy.

The boat rocked and swayed as it approached the water-fall. Cameras clicked, seagulls cried, and Beth realised that her fears were quite unfounded; in fact the ride was exhilarat-ing and she didn't want it to end. She turned around to Liam and kissed him. His face was wet in the misty air.

"I love it!"

He reached down, kissed her lips, and saw the love of life was back in her eyes. She felt his lips touch hers, and thought to herself that he probably had been right; now there was nothing left in the world that she could not accomplish if she just set her mind to it.

CHAPTER 28 - BETH

SHE HAD DEBATED long and hard as to whether she should wear the traditional white gown. She was a mother of two children and no longer in the first flush of youth, but somehow Beth still felt as though Edwin had cheated her out of her rightful wedding. Eventually without too much resistance she had yielded to her mother and Amy's suggestions and had settled on an ivory silk and lace off the shoulder creation with a matching bolero, unwilling to show too much flesh. As she let her mother finish applying unfamiliar make-up, Beth smiled at Amy, already proficient at supervising her little brother as he pulled himself up and moved around the furniture on unsteady toddler legs.

"It'll be time to put on your bridesmaid's dress in a minute, darling." Beth held out her hand to steady her son. "Granny will take Joss."

"I can look after him." Amy, ever mindful of the baby falling, kneeled down and positioned herself behind him.

"I know you can, but it's time to make yourself even lovelier than you are already. The car will be here shortly to take us to the church."

"Where's Daddy?" Amy picked Joss up and hugged him.

"He's been staying with Grandad Darrah. It's unlucky for a bride and groom to see each other before the wedding." Beth admired herself in the mirror. "Thanks Mum, you've done a grand job; the foundation makes all the difference."

"You look absolutely radiant." Sally Nichols smiled at her daughter. "I'll take Joss and head off to the church with Auntie Sue. Dad's waiting for you downstairs when you're ready."

The wasted years slipped away as Beth fastened the tiny pearl buttons at the back of Amy's long, layered pale pink chiffon dress.

"You're beautiful, you look so grown up." She smiled at her daughter. "Let me brush your hair."

Beth undid the long blonde plait, and Amy's hair cascaded in rivulets to her waist. As she brushed the shimmering waves she felt a pang of regret for her own lost tresses.

"Don't ever cut your hair." She sighed and kissed the top of her daughter's head. "Pick up your bouquet and wait downstairs with Grandpa now while I get ready."

She relished the few minutes alone before stepping into her wedding dress. Taking off her dressing gown and slipping on new matching lacy underwear and a floor-length petticoat, Beth looked at herself again in the mirror. There *were* a few extra lines on her face, but then she realised how a lack of sunshine during her confinement had probably gone some way in having the strangely positive effect of keeping her complexion relatively smooth.

The gown was luxuriant; she felt like a million dollars as she fastened the zip. She gave a secret smile to herself knowing that her stockings and blue garters would cause Liam to be pleasantly surprised after the festivities had ended.

She patted her hair into place. The elfin cut had now lengthened into a not unattractive bob. Managing to eschew her mother's wish for a veil, Beth fastened the ivory fascinator in place, slipped into somewhat uncomfortable ivory stilettos, and nodded to herself in the mirror at the finished product.

She was ready to be married.

Picking up her bouquet of pink and white carnations, she walked carefully down the stairs, lifting up the hem of her dress slightly. She smiled at her father and Amy, waiting patiently by the front door.

"You look stunning." Robert Nichols nodded approvingly at his daughter. "Liam's a lucky man."

"Thanks Dad; I'm getting nervous now."

"The car's outside. Mum's gone on ahead." Robert opened the door. "Ready?"

"As ready as I'll ever be." She exhaled a shaky breath.

"Let's go then."

The church was packed with relatives she had not seen for more than ten years. As she stood at the back of the church holding her father's arm and waiting for her cue, Beth could see that not one pew remained empty. At the last minute just as the organ began to play, she bent forward and whispered in Amy's ear.

"Walk in front of me and not behind. Daddy will feel more at home; it's how they do weddings in Canada."

When she began the interminable walk to the altar and he turned around and gave her *that* smile, her shakiness seemed to disappear in a flash, enabling her to finally enjoy their wedding day which she had thought about for so long through the endless days and nights in the house without windows.

CHAPTER 29 – JOSS

THE BELL SOUNDED for the end of lessons, and Joss Darrah heaved a sigh of relief. Double science on a Friday afternoon sucked; especially when he knew Tara Lambert had given up the subject in favour of music, and would now be waiting outside the school for her lift home. Mrs Lambert was always late, and if only Mr Bruton would shut the fuck up then it might be possible to leg it around the sixth form block, run along past the tennis courts, and then reach the entrance gates just in time to speak two words to Tara before her mother arrived. At this rate though he would have to wait until Monday to convince the most beautiful girl in his class that he actually did exist; not that she seemed to care a jot if he did or if he didn't.

But first there was the weekend's homework task to copy down ready for Monday. Joss likened Mr Bruton's frizzy ginger hair to an explosion. The teacher began to write on the whiteboard in his irritatingly slow way: 'To research the laws of genetic inheritance and apply it to your own family'.

Joss *tutted* with annoyance, scribbled down the work to be done, packed his rucksack, and quickly elbowed his way out of the classroom.

"You're wasting your time, dickhead. She's got the hots for Daniel Summerlee." Joss turned around as he heard the voice of his best friend Benny Cashman behind him.

"Up yours, Cashman!" Joss swung his rucksack to make contact with Benny's head.

"I'll knock for you tomorrow, that is if you're not too busy giving her one!" Benny laughed as he watched his friend disappear.

By the time he had made it to the front gates the most beautiful girl in his class and her mother were driving off in a cloud of exhaust fumes. He gazed at the back of Tara's head, unsuccessfully willing her to turn around and look at him.

"Bollocks!"

He kicked stones along the street as he walked home. One flew up and left a small dent in a Mini Cooper parked by the side of the road. Joss ran the few streets home as fast as his legs could carry him.

"You're a bit later today." Beth, his mother, appeared in the hallway.

"I was talking to Benny." "You're always talking to Benny." "He's coming round tomorrow."

"As long as you do your homework first."

"It's boring though. I've got to read about the laws of inheritance and then write about it."

"Is that for sociology?"

Joss noticed that his mother suddenly had one of those inscrutable looks on her face.

"No, for science."

"Well, it's up to you of course, but Benny doesn't come in until after you've done it."

"Cheers, Mum."

Flinging the hated rucksack onto his bed, Joss picked up his iPad, typed the password 'taralambert', and smiled at Benny's message.

'What did she say?'

The possibilities were endless. Finally he decided on the best one.

'She says she'll go out with me and that you're a wanker.'

While he waited for the inevitable pithy response he decided to take his mother's advice and please Bombhead Bruton at the same time. He typed 'laws of inheritance' into the Internet browser and sighed with boredom as he read about Gregor Mendel's experiments with pea plants in the 1850's.

'Each inherited trait is defined by a gene pair. Parental genes are randomly separated to the sex cells so that sex cells contain only one gene of the pair. Offspring therefore inherit one genetic allele from each parent when sex cells unite in fertilization.'

He yawned and imagined his and Tara's sex cells uniting in fertilisation. *Fat chance!*

'An organism with alternate forms of a gene will express the form that is dominant. Mendel's laws still apply today, for example in the form of dominant and recessive genes for a person's eye colour and hair colour.'

His iPad pinged with an incoming message.

'You're a twat. See ya tomoz.'

Joss laughed and made another Internet search on dominant eye colour.

'The iris of the eye has pigmentation that determines a person's eye colour. A person with blue or light grey eyes does not have as much pigmentation as a person with brown or black eyes. The amount of pigmentation in the iris is determined genetically. The gene for brown eyes is dominant over the recessive gene for blue, grey, or hazel eyes. Thus it is likely that two blue eyed parents will produce a blue eyed child, but if one parent has brown eyes then it is likely the child will have brown eyes, as the gene for brown eyes is dominant.'

Something about the last sentence did not feel right. He'd never really thought about it before, but now a tiny doubt had begun to nag. He read it a second time, and then realised what was wrong.

His mother's eyes were light grey. His father's eyes were blue. His sister Amy had blue eyes. They were all fair-haired!

He stood up, walked over to the mirror on the wall and looked at himself. The eyes that stared back at him were dark brown, almost black; the same colour as his hair.

CHAPTER 30 - JOSS

"YOU'RE QUIET TONIGHT Joss. Bad day at school?" Liam Darrah sprinkled some parmesan cheese onto his lasa-gna and poured himself a glass of wine.

"Amy will be home soon for the Easter break. I'm sure you two will have lots to catch up on." Beth smiled at her son as he toyed unenthusiastically with his dinner.

"I'm having a bit of trouble with my homework."

"You need some help, eh?" Liam's fork stopped halfway to his mouth.

"I think so. I don't understand how Mendel's law of inheritance relates to our family."

Joss was aware of a small, almost imperceptible glance passing between his parents.

"What's your question?" Beth put down her knife and fork.

"How have you and Dad produced someone like me? According to what I've read you both have the recessive gene for blue or grey eyes. Amy has straight fair hair and the same colour eyes as Dad, but look at me; I've got brown wavy hair and black eyes. It just doesn't make sense." Joss sighed and idly put some pasta onto his fork.

"Well, sometimes a baby inherits traits from his grand-parents or great-grandparents." Beth was relieved her son couldn't tell how fast her heart was racing.

"None of my grandparents are as dark as I am."

The rest of the meal passed in silence. Joss felt some-how on edge. He heard his parents start talking in a low voice to each other as soon as he went back upstairs to his room. As he went over his research to try and find some-thing that perhaps he'd failed to understand, he heard a knock.

"Yo!"

He looked up to find his parents standing in the door-way.

"Joss, Dad and I have been talking, and there's some-thing we need to tell you."

"What?" He was taken aback by his mother's tone of voice.

"Well, it's something we should have told you a long time ago, but now you're growing up and asking questions, it's not fair to keep you in the dark."

Joss felt his stomach churning, and he suddenly felt queasy. He definitely did not want to hear what his mother had to say.

"You don't have to tell me. It's cool." He felt sick. "Dad loves you very much, as much as I do. He's brought you up to be the fine boy that you are today. We're both very proud of you."

Something nasty was coming right at him.

"What's wrong with Dad? Is he sick?"

His dad had cancer! He was going to die! Joss felt tears forming at the back of his eyes.

"No, he's fine. It's just that Dad is your father in every sense of the word, but he is not your biological father. As you say it's very true that both of us could not produce a child as dark as yourself. You have your biological father's colouring."

The sudden relief that his father was not close to death gave Joss a feeling of wild euphoria. He lay back on the bed and closed his eyes. *His dad was ok!*

"So what happened then? Where's my real dad now?" He sat back up, curious. *Had his mother had an affair?*

"I think things might best be left as they are." Liam placed an arm protectively across Beth's shoulders.

"No, he has a right to know. Joss, I'm just so sorry. As your mother I should have told you sooner." Beth walked towards the bed, sat down, and put an arm around her son.

"Told me that you've had an affair? Is that it?" Joss flinched from her embrace.

"I never had an affair. I was engaged to be married to Dad and was newly pregnant with Amy, but was then abducted by your biological father and held prisoner for nearly ten years. Amy never mentioned it to you because she hates the sight of him and also we told her not to. We thought it best that you didn't find out. Your father's name is Edwin Evans, but you were registered with my surname. When Dad and I married we changed both you and Amy's surnames to Darrah."

Joss jumped up and began pacing about the room.

"How could you not tell me? I had a right to know!"

"We're sorry. We wanted to forget the heartache and start anew." Liam was stung by the hurt in the boy's eyes. "We've brought you and Amy up the same. We love you both, but we didn't want to be reminded of what had gone on before."

"Where's my father now then?" Joss stood tall and threatening in front of his mother.

"Your father is here in the room with us, darling." Beth stood up to face her son. "But your biological father has been a resident of Holmleas Psychiatric Hospital for the Criminally Insane in Croydon, for the past 11 years.

The lasagna tasted vile at the back of his throat. Joss just managed to get to the bathroom in time. He dropped to his knees and emptied his stomach contents into the toilet bowl. He was aware of his father's warm hand rubbing his back and of his soft Canadian accent in his ears.

"You'll feel better now. Don't worry. Mom and I are here for you. We'll always be here for you."

He rinsed his mouth at the sink and went back to lie on his bed.

"Leave me alone, please." He put his face in his pillow and tried to shut out the world.

CHAPTER 31 - JOSS

"I'M NOT GOING to Bombhead's class."

"Bunking off again?" Benny looked at his friend and laughed.

"I haven't done any homework. I'll wait for you at the front gate. Tell him I went home sick."

"Ok. See you later."

Joss passed the entire science period sitting in his favourite cubicle in the boys' toilets, still trying to get his head around his mother's recent revelations. When he heard the bell ring for the end of the final lesson he joined the mass exodus of teenagers making their way to the front gate. To his surprise Tara Lambert was already waiting there for her mother.

"I saw you sneaking out of the toilets, Joss."

"Yeah, well, I hadn't done any homework." *He'd have to be more careful next time.*

"Don't worry, I won't grass you up."

"Cheers." He felt a tingling in his groin at her nearness, and pulled his jacket over his growing erection.

"Fuck off, Darrah." Daniel Summerlee, already with a man's muscly body, loomed large as he stood himself in-between Joss and Tara.

Joss had had enough. The secret he now had to bear was beginning to weigh him down.

"Fuck off yourself!"

He pushed Summerlee's chest hard with both hands. The boy lost his balance and fell backwards onto the stony ground.

"You're dead meat, Darrah!" Summerlee was back up on his feet, fists flailing in anger.

Joss could see he was no match for the youth, already lifting sizeable weights at the gym. Ducking a left hook he did the only thing he could think of to save himself; he kicked Summerlee hard in the groin, who went down like the proverbial sack of potatoes. Aware of Tara's gaze of admiration, he walked away with his head held high.

"Wait for me!" Benny ran up behind him, laughing. "Summerlee's still on the floor, the prick."

"Does this face look bothered?"

"You'll better watch yourself at school tomorrow."

"I'm not going. I'll give him a day to cool off. Bunk off with me if you like. Mum and Dad will be at the hospital. We'll have the house to ourselves until at least three o'clock."

"Yeah? I know how to access a good porn site."

"Everybody does. It's easy!" Joss threw Benny a punch.

"My brother's got a black box that he attaches to his computer. He makes a phone call, puts in a code and hey presto, there's more porn than you can shake your dick at. It's great. The code runs out after a week and then he pays for another one. I know where he's written it down. I'll bring the machine round. He won't miss it during the day."

Joss laughed.

"I'll hide out in the park until 9.30. Come round after that."

"You're on. See you in the morning!" Benny sloped off in the opposite direction.

His mother seemed agitated as soon as he returned home.

"Joss, have you been fighting? I've just had a phone call from the school. Mrs Summerlee has had to take Daniel to the Accident and Emergency Department. You're lucky she's not pressing any charges."

"He must be putting it on. I didn't hit him that hard!"

"His parents are not pleased. I think you owe Daniel an apology"

He felt a sinking feeling in the pit of his stomach.

"He started it. I wasn't doing anything."

"Well you've certainly done something. The boy's injured."

"Only his pride. I kicked him in the nuts."

"You're coming with us to his house to apologise and sort this out later on."

"Jeez Mum! No! It was his fault!" Joss ran up to his room and slammed the door.

He laid on his bed simmering with anger, and thought about what his real father was like. What might he have done under the same circumstances? Would he have killed Summerlee? Would ten men have been needed to hold him off? Joss got up and looked at himself in the mirror again. He looked nothing like his mother or Amy; he was his father's son.

Where was Croydon? He hadn't the first clue. How far away was it from Norwich? He typed Croydon into his iPad. The search came back describing the largest borough on the outskirts of London; population about 370,000. One of those was his dad.

He struggled to remember the name of the institution. Eventually he searched for hospitals for the criminally insane in Croydon. One came back; Holmleas, Whitgift Road, Ardlington, Croydon, Surrey.

That was the one!

He had no idea how he was going to get there, but someday soon he knew he would be making the journey to Surrey.

CHAPTER 32 - JOSS

"HAVE YOU BEEN smoking in here?"

Beth shivered and closed her son's bedroom window. She wondered whether Benjamin Cashman was having an undesirable influence on Joss.

"Where would I get any cigarettes from?" Joss smiled inwardly and mentally gave thanks to Benny's resourceful brother Jimmy.

"How long have you been home?" "Oh, only about half an hour." "Has Benny been round here?" "No."

Beth sighed at the sight of her son lying on his bed at three thirty in the afternoon, and found it hard to ignore yet more evidence of another day spent truanting from school with Benny; four dirty coffee cups, empty fish and chip wrappers, and two plates still with the remains of sandwiches made with the roast chicken she was keeping for tomorrow.

"I can see with my own eyes that you haven't been to school again today. The room stinks of cigarette smoke despite the force 8 gale that you had blowing in through your window. You're lucky the smoke alarms didn't activate. Your exams are coming up in a few months, and here you are frittering your time away."

"Leave it out, Mum. I'll go to school tomorrow. Just give me a break."

"Dad will hear about this when he comes in."

"How can he hear about it if he's banged up?" Joss regretted the outburst as soon as he saw his mother's face blanch.

"How dare you even mention that man's name! Do you want to know just what he did to me? Do you?" Beth was suddenly overcome with a white-hot fury coursing through her veins.

Joss turned over onto his front, put his head in the pillow, and tried to shut out the sound of his mother's whining voice. His dad had probably done exactly what the Kitten Sisters had had done to them on Jimmy's movie machine that afternoon. They seemed to enjoy the experience; in fact the blonde one definitely did. He wondered how it would feel doing it to Tara Lambert.

The memory foam sank lower as his mother came to sit next to him on the bed. He felt her hand touch his hair.

"I know you've had a shock, Joss, and I know I should have told you sooner. I apologise for that. But it's something I wanted to bury in the past. He was an evil man with a twisted mind. It's not something that I wanted to be reminded of."

Joss lifted his face from the pillow but did not turn around.

"Sorry Mum, but I can't stop thinking about him. I just can't pretend nothing's happened and carry on like before.

He's my dad, and I want to know more about him. I want to see what he looks like; if I look like him or not. I want to hear his voice. I want to visit him in prison. I want to meet him." *There….it was out!* He was glad he couldn't see his mother's face at that precise moment. He let his head sink down again as he listened to his pounding heart.

The silence in the room was deafening. He heard the ticking of one of the many old-fashioned clocks that were on nearly every wall in the house. At one point he thought he heard a sob. Eventually he felt his mother move from the bed. He listened intently for her reply, but she walked out of his bedroom without speaking another word.

He sat up and reached for his iPad. The previous search was still there. He read that any visitors to Holmleas must inform Reception at least five days in advance. No visits were allowed on Mondays, Tuesdays or Fridays, and there was a special visiting room for children. Up to three people over the age of 16 could sit with the patient at one of the 15 tables available in the main visitors' area between 2 – 4 pm every Wednesday, Thursday, Saturday or Sunday afternoon. Refreshments and toilets were available. He was further informed that Holmleas had been built in 2001 on the site of the previous Ardlington council estate, and was on bus route 465, about a 30 minute journey out of East Croydon Station.

Today was Tuesday. If he could find a way of getting there he could phone the hospital right now and give them his name. He would be able to meet his father on Sunday afternoon!

"How much is a return journey from Norwich train station to East Croydon?" *The smart bastard phone would know.*

Back came the robotic voice.

"One hundred and eight pounds and seventy pence. The journey will take three hours and twenty minutes."

Smart bastard.

"Will you have sex with me?"

"I hardly know you."

"Dial Holmleas Hospital for the Criminally Insane." "If you ask nicely."

"Dial Holmleas Hospital for the Criminally Insane *please.*"

"Dialling."

Bastard phone!

"Good afternoon. Holmleas." The female voice on the other end of the phone sounded to Joss as though she had a silver spoon up her arse.

"My name is Joss Darrah. I would like to visit Edwin Evans on Sunday please."

"What is your relationship to Mr Evans?" "I'm his son."

There was a brief silence at the other end as the plummy voice recovered from the shock.

"Leave me your details and I will phone you back directly if Mr Evans agrees to receive visitors."

Joss ended the call on a high. Now all that was needed was to obtain about two hundred pounds. A small smile played about his lips as he realised that getting the money would be easier than taking candy from a baby.

He recognised the knock at his bedroom door.

"Mom tells me you haven't been to school today."

Joss looked at the man whom for 16 years he had thought of as his father.

"Daniel Summerlee says I'm dead meat. Would you go, knowing you're going to get beaten up?"

"I'll speak to the head teacher."

"It won't make any difference. He'll wait until we're out of the school gates."

"Then I'll come and pick you up in the car."

"Leave it Dad. I'll sort it." Joss sighed and wished the plummy woman would phone him back.

"Mom also tells me that you're talking about visiting Edwin Evans. It would break her heart if you did that. I strongly advise against it."

"I've changed my mind. It's not a good idea." The lie slid effortlessly off his tongue.

"Glad you've seen sense, son. He put your mother and sister through hell. Mom in particular took years to recover." Joss felt the phone begin to vibrate in his pocket. He took it out and looked at the screen.

"It's Tara Lambert calling. I think I might have a hot date."

"Then I'll leave you to it." Liam smiled.

"Thanks Dad."

He waited until the bedroom door closed and then answered the call from the hospital.

"May I speak to Joss Darrah please?" The silver spoon had been stuck even further up.

"Yeah, speaking."

"You called regarding visiting Edwin Evans?"

"That's right."

"I'm sorry to tell you that Mr Evans has requested no visitors at this time."

"What?" Joss sat up on his bed.

"No visitors. Mr Evans was quite insistent."

"But I'm his son!"

"If the patient does not want any visitors then I'm afraid there's nothing I can do."

Joss ended the call, angry at tears that were already stinging his eyes. *Why did his dad not want to meet him? It made no sense at all!*

The disappointment was more than he could bear. He put his head in his hands and let the bitter tears fall. He sighed as he remembered his grandmother's words: *If at first you don't succeed, try, try, and try again.*

He sniffed and wiped his eyes.

He would not give up. He would get to meet his father one way or another.

CHAPTER 33 - JOSS

JOSS TOOK HIS seat for registration. A breathy voice in his ear coming from behind made him shiver.

"Hey Joss. You'd better watch out for Daniel. He was mad as anything yesterday. Good thing you weren't at school." Tara leaned back in her chair as Joss looked around.

"He's a prat. I'll get Loaf on my side." Joss smiled at the vision of loveliness twirling a strand of black hair around a finger. "Want to come round mine after school?"

"Can't. Mum's picking me up for my piano lesson."

"Shit."

"Try again, Darrah."

"What about Friday?   I'll tell Mum you're coming for tea."

"Ok."

Joss smiled and felt a warm glow inside. As he turned around he saw Daniel Summerlee holding up a piece of paper in his direction. He read the child-like writing.

Dead meat.

He stared at Summerlee as hard as he could without blinking. The stare was returned.

"Nice to see you back, Joss. How are we today?" Elise Vane tried her best to muster up enough bonhomie to greet her most enthusiastic truant.

"Better thanks, Mrs Vane." Joss unwillingly took his gaze off Summerlee to look at his form mistress.

"I'll take registration and then I've got you all for English. Mr Sanders is off sick today."

Elise could hear an almost decipherable groan at the students' sure and certain knowledge that there would be extra English homework that evening.

"Hey, Loaf!" Joss whispered to the huge dense-looking teenage boy sitting to his left who had groaned the loudest.

Carl Baker glanced to his right.

"What?"

"I'll do your English homework for you if you help me out with something."

"Yeah ok."

"Meet you back here at break."

Joss smiled again.   The day was starting out very well. *What a good thing that Loaf could hardly read a word.*

The boy was waiting as soon as Joss returned to the classroom.

"Mrs Vane's given us that fucking essay to do. I can't do it, Joss."

"I know, but I can. I've got something you can do instead while I'm doing your essay."

"What's that?"

"Frighten off Summerlee. He's getting on my tits."

"Yeah, I can do that. That's well easy." Loaf gave a sinister smile and cracked his knuckles.

"Good man. I'll do your English Literature one as well, 'cos it might take you a few tries."

"Nah. I'll scare the shit out of him straight away!"

"He won't do anything until later when we're out of the school gates."

"I'll be waiting. Cheers for the essay."

Joss breathed a sigh of relief. *Loaf was as thick as shit, but it was good to get him on your side for times such as these.*

There was no way out of the school except through the front gates. His heart began to beat faster as he saw Summerlee waiting for him outside at the end of the day. He took a second look as he tried to blend in with the exiting students jamming the approach to the gates, but this time Summerlee was not alone; Loaf was there with him. Joss breathed a sigh of relief as he saw the huge frame towering over his arch enemy. By the time he had got to the gates only Loaf was waiting, cracking his knuckles.

"He's scared as fuck now."

"Cheers, Loaf. I owe you one."

"Yeah, you owe me an essay."

"I'll do it tonight with mine."

Joss fervently hoped that Summerlee would not find out about his date with Tara. If he did there would be hell to pay.

Turning the key in the lock he was surprised when his mother appeared in the hallway.

"Good day at school?"

"Yeah, great. Why are you home so early today?"

"The last patient didn't turn up."

"Oh. Is it ok if Tara Lambert comes to tea on Friday?"

"Of course. You can sit in the den with her and play your music afterwards."

"Oh Mum!"

"Not in the bedroom. No." "The age of consent is 15 now!"

"She won't be consenting to anything in my house." *Shit!*

Joss skulked upstairs and flung himself on his bed. There were two messages from Benny on his phone. He up-dated his friend with the latest news regarding Tara and Summerlee, but then the two English essays started to prey on his mind.

Bollocks! However, they had to be done. Loaf could hardly read his own name. Time to get to work. His mother would be well impressed at his diligence.

CHAPTER 34 - JOSS

"THAT WAS A lovely meal Mrs Darrah. Shall I help you clear the table?" Tara began piling plates one on top of the other.

"Thanks for the offer, but there's no need. You and Joss go into the den."

"Cheers, Mum." Joss had half a mind to brazen it out and take Tara upstairs, just to find out if his mother would make a scene.

"Where's the den?" Tara looked around appreciatively at the décor.

"It's next door. Come on." Joss gave his mother a hard stare.

"Wow! What a lovely room!" Tara gazed at the 52" TV screen and media console.

"It's mine and Amy's, and Toby's too when he's over here."

"Who's Amy and Toby?"

"Amy's my sister. She's in the last year of medical school. She'll be home at Easter. Her fiancée Paul is a doctor as well, in fact all my family are doctors except Toby, my step-brother. He lives in Canada and he's really, really cool. He plays guitar in a rock band out there."

"Which one?"

"They're called Kick & Scream."

"Wow! I've heard of them. I didn't know the guitarist was your brother."

He's not!

Tara picked up a 7 string Ibanez from its stand.

"Is this Toby's?"

"Yeah. He plays it all the time when he's here. I can't play a note though."

"Your dad's really good-looking."

"He's not my dad." *No!* Joss could have bitten his tongue at the mistake.

Tara was quick on the uptake.

"What do you mean, he's not your dad?"

"Er... my real dad lives in Croydon. They're divorced."

"I didn't know that. Where's Croydon?"

"It's in Surrey. Don't tell anyone though."

"Why not?"

"I don't want you to."

"Okay."

"Why do you call him Dad then if he's not your dad?" "I've always called him that."

Tara moved around the room, looking at posters on the walls.

"Can we watch a film?"

"Sure. I'll turn on the console and you can pick one."

Joss was disappointed when Tara chose one of Amy's romances he had no interest in. She came and sat down next to him and he felt himself becoming aroused at her nearness. He put an arm around the back of the sofa and a magazine on his lap.

"You're cool, Joss Darrah."

Tara settled back onto the sofa and his fingers touched her hair. He wanted to burst with happiness at the compliment. He brought his arm around to encircle her shoulders.

"This is a great evening. I'm really enjoying myself." Tara lifted her face to his and brushed his lips with hers.

"Will you go out with me?" Joss, emboldened and inflamed with passion, kissed her mouth and touched her tongue with his own.

"Yeah. I'll go out with you."

He didn't care that the film sucked big time; he felt about ten feet tall. Just sitting on the sofa with the girl of his dreams was enough to make him forget momentarily that his dad didn't want to get to know him.

She snuggled up closer, and he looked down at the curve of her breasts under her thin jumper as the film droned on.

"Joss; Mrs Lambert is here to pick up Tara."

He jumped at the sound of his mother's voice at the door. As he saw her tactfully withdraw, Tara disentangled herself from his embrace and smoothed down her skirt.

"I'm working tomorrow at the hairdressers, but I'll ask Mum if you can come round in the evening. I'll phone and let you know."

"Great."

With a waft of perfume she was gone. Joss sat back, closed his eyes, and remembered the warmth of her body against his. The film they had been watching together was still running, and with a sigh he turned off the console.

"She seems like a nice girl." Liam smiled as Joss came into the living room.

"She is. I might be going round her place tomorrow."

"Will her parents be there?" His mother was instantly on the alert.

"Don't worry Mum. I'm sure we'll be spied on all the time."

"Mum is concerned, that's all. You know how mothers are."

Joss looked at the man he used to think of as his father.

"Dad; what did you get up to when you were sixteen? Did Granny spy on you?"

"All the time."

"Did it make you mad as hell?"

"Sure did. But as I grew older I realized she was just looking out for me until I was wise enough to look out for myself."

"Are you saying I'm stupid?" Joss was instantly on the defensive.

"Not at all. You're quite the opposite. I'm saying that Granny was just looking out for me."

Joss looked into the smiling blue eyes that were nothing like his own. He wanted to punch his dad on the nose. The dad that was never his father in the first place, and never would be again.

As he walked upstairs to his room the phone vibrated in his pocket. When he looked at the screen he was surprised to see Holmleas' name appear. He closed his bedroom door for privacy.

"Hello."

"Can I speak to Joss Darrah please?" A male voice spoke this time.

"Speaking."

"This is just to let you know that Mr Evans has changed his mind. He says you can visit him tomorrow. Visiting hours in the afternoon are two o'clock until four o'clock."

His head spun for a moment at the news. Finally he managed to put a sentence together:

"Tell him I'll be there."

CHAPTER 35 - JOSS

THE PHONE VIBRATED under his pillow at 3am, just as he had planned. Rubbing his eyes, Joss got out of bed and pulled on a dressing gown. Making sure to avoid the one creaking floorboard on the landing, he crept downstairs, stepped over the pressure pad by the front door and turned off the burglar alarm. Making his way along the hallway to the office he hoped his dad's usual wad of notes would still be in the cash box in the desk drawer. He took the key from under a book on the shelf above.

Yes! He counted out £150 in twenty and ten pound notes and stuffed them into his dressing gown pocket. The wad looked decidedly thinner as he locked up the cash box again and replaced the key, but at that particular moment he did not care at all. Closing the office door quietly, he crept back up the hallway and turned the burglar alarm back on. There was a succession of rapid beeps as it sprang back to life, and Joss held his breath as he knew his mother was a very light sleeper.

When no footsteps could be heard in the main bedroom, he tiptoed upstairs, stepped over the noisy floorboard, and with a sigh of relief crept into his bedroom. He took the notes out of his pocket and placed them in the front zipped compartment of his rucksack. He then climbed back into bed and slept fitfully until he heard his parents getting up for their Saturday morning clinics.

"Morning Joss. Have you got anything planned today?" His mother passed him some hot toast.

"Yeah. I'm going into Norwich with Tara, and then I'm going back to her place at Eaton for dinner later on."

"Yes, I swapped addresses and phone numbers with Tara's mother yesterday. It's nice out that way."

"Mum, you don't have to keep ringing her up every five minutes to check on me. I'll get the bus there and her mum will give me a lift back tonight."

"I won't ring, it's just in case of an emergency so I know where you are. Call if you need anything. We're always on the other end of the phone, you know that."

"Yeah." *His mother was crazy; always worried that something would happen.*

Waiting impatiently for his parents to leave the house, Joss synched the train journey and directions to the hospital from his iPad to his phone, and then raided the kitchen for extra food to fill his rucksack with on hearing their car pulling out of the driveway. He made it to the station in ten minutes.

"Return ticket to East Croydon please. I'm paying cash."

"Nobody pays with cash these days." The old station master looked surprised to receive a handful of twenty pound notes.

"I do. I haven't got a bank account."

"Okay. Well, when you get to Liverpool Street you get the Central line tube to Bank, and then the Northern line to London Bridge. After that you have to get the overland from London Bridge to East Croydon."

"That's exactly what it says on my phone."

"Why am I needed here I ask myself?"

"You're not. Cheers Granddad." Joss took the ticket. "Which platform?"

"I thought I wasn't wanted?"

"Just for today, and then you can retire."

"Platform three. Next train in. Express." *Smart arse.*

He had been on a train only once before in his whole life. He thought back and remembered going with his parents and Toby to London a couple of years' ago in the summer holidays. *Toby had been a right arsehole and had wanted to spend all the time looking around boring music shops in Denmark Street.*

His heart beat faster as he heard the train approaching. Stepping into a carriage, he closed the door, took off his rucksack, and settled into a corner seat.

He was on his way!

He remembered to send a message to Tara.

'Gone to Croydon to see my dad. Meet up tomoz."

The stations flashed past: Diss, Ipswich, Manningtree and Colchester. Before too long he was in the very heart of London. At the Liverpool Street terminal he got out of the train and looked around, overawed by the size of the station and the amount of people rushing to and fro. Putting his ticket into the slot on the security barrier at the entrance to the tube station, he felt relieved when the gate opened to let him through. As he travelled down in the escalator towards the Central line he wrinkled his nose at the smell, and remembered he hadn't liked it much the previous time either.

A whooshing sound heralded the arrival of the train, full of shoppers and tourists out for the day in London. There was nowhere to sit. Joss hung onto one of the overhead straps until he arrived at Bank. The Northern line was somewhat less crowded, and he found a seat next to a couple of Japanese tourists who gabbled away incomprehensively until he could thankfully escape at London Bridge.

He could not stop the butterflies in his stomach on the journey to East Croydon. He checked the number of the bus again on his phone. There was a message from Tara.

'Ta for the message. CU tomoz. X'

He smiled at the kiss, and ate a piece of his mother's apple strudel, washing it down with some water out of a plastic bottle he remembered to put in the side pocket of his rucksack. By the time the train pulled into the station he was feeling queasy with nervousness. After finding the men's room he walked outside and joined the queue for the 465 bus. He looked down at his phone. It was 1.24; exactly four hours since he had left Norwich. He would be face to face with his real dad in little more than half an hour's time.

The double decker bus travelled slowly through the centre of Croydon, slowing down at every bus stop along the way to pick up frazzled shoppers laden with a multitude of bags and possessions. By the time it had reached Shirley Hills the majority of passengers had alighted, leaving only Joss and two other women sitting downstairs. The women stayed on until Ardlington, stepping off behind Joss as the bus pulled up in front of the hospital.

The women were obviously visiting somebody, as they seemed to know where to go. Joss walked slowly behind them, watching them showing some sort of paperwork to the man standing in front of a 15 foot high main door that was closed and bolted, but with a smaller open door on the right hand side built into it. The women walked through the smaller opening, which the guard then closed and locked.

"Afternoon, son. Can I see your visitors' pass please?"

Joss felt his heart sink into his boots.

"I haven't got one. Somebody phoned me yesterday to tell me my dad wanted to see me today."

"Who's your dad?"

"Edwin Evans."

"Ah yes, that was me. He changed his mind. Next time you'll need to apply for a pass at least five days in advance."

"Yeah, sorry. There wasn't time to get one."

"Go straight on and through the door on your left at the end of the courtyard. Someone will show you where to go from there."

The guard opened the door and Joss stepped through the opening and into a pleasant courtyard with fountains on either side cascading into two shallow ponds, each containing several large goldfish. Cherry trees covered in pink blossom fringed the edges of the courtyard, and numerous benches had been built beneath the trees. The whole scene was tranquil, and Joss felt like resting on one of the seats for a while. However, visiting time was only until four o'clock, and it was already past two.

His heart began to pound in his chest when he saw the open door at the other end of the courtyard. A member of staff was there to direct him to the visitors' area, a short walk away down a corridor painted a pale yellow. Joss saw several patients seated at tables with their visitors. The two women he'd seen on the bus were seated either side of a thin teenage girl, and all three seemed to be talking at the same time.

"I've come to see Edwin Evans."

"You need to leave that rucksack here with me, but he's over there."

The burly guard behind his desk pointed over to a man sitting alone at a table on the far side of the room, staring straight at him. Joss reasoned the man to be in his early sixties. He had grey hair and a grey beard and his body seemed thin under a loose fitting dark blue track suit. Joss could see the facial features were unmistakably those of himself in fifty years' time. He took off his rucksack, gave it to the guard, and walked around the other tables towards the man.

"Hello." Joss was lost for any more words at the sight of his father.

The man continued staring at him without speaking. Joss sat down opposite and tried to think of something to say.

"I'm Joss. I'm your son. My mother is Beth."

"What kind of a fucking name is Joss?"

"It's short for Jocelyn. Yeah, I hate it as well. It sucks." Joss was pleased to have elicited some sort of response from his father.

"I read about a Jocelyn in a book I once had as a kid. I gave it to your sister. Is she here?" Evans looked towards the door.

"No. Just me. Amy kept the book for years, but I don't know where it is now."

"She'd better not have chucked it away. I told her to look after it." The voice sounded threatening. "What do you want?"

"I just wanted to meet you. That's all." Joss smiled and looked into inscrutable coal black eyes the image of his own.

"Well, now you have you'll piss off I suppose."

"I wouldn't mind a cup of tea first. I've been travelling for four hours."

"Where do you live then? Back of bloody beyond?"

Joss laughed nervously and twisted his hands together.

"No. We live in Norwich, near the station."

"I first saw your mother in Norwich. I was in hospital. She had long blonde hair. An angel of mercy. That's what she was. An angel of mercy." Evans' voice softened. "I think about her every day. I'm only alive now because I know I'll see her again. I'd have topped myself otherwise."

"Well, she's older and her hair's short and grey now. It's always been short as far as I can recall. Is that the tea trolley?" Joss had not travelled for four hours to talk about his mother.

"Tell her to grow it!" Evans thumped his fist on the table. "She must not have it cut!"

The guard stood up from his desk and looked across. Joss felt a wave of fear rush through his body.

"It's ok Dad, I'll tell her." He moved away and took two cups of tea from the trolley, giving one to his father.

"I have three sugars."

"Ok. Give me the cup again and I'll put them in."

Joss added three heaped teaspoons of sugar to his father's tea. Evans' bad temper disappeared as quickly as it had arrived on being handed the sweet, steaming liquid.

"When's your mother coming to see me?" He whined. "You're the first visitor that's come since I've been here."

"Mum's married now. My stepfather wouldn't want her to come." Try as he might, Joss could not seem to drag the conversation away from his mother.

"If it wasn't for you being born, you little shit, she'd still be home with me." Evans hissed softly between closed teeth, sipped some tea, and all the while his black eyes bored into Joss. "They got me while I waited outside for her to be wheeled out of the operating theatre. This is all your fucking fault. I should have kept her with me then you would have died. It's the biggest mistake I ever made, taking her to that place."

Joss felt shocked and uncomfortable. The meeting was not going the way he'd planned. His father should have been pleased to see him after sixteen years.

"Tell that prick his days are numbered. When I get out of this fucking hospital I'm coming for him. I take my medications like I'm told. I'm a good boy. My six-monthly assessment is coming round soon. I'll be good and will be out of here and on my way to Norwich to get my Beth before you can say 'Jack shit'."

Joss found his father's eyes mesmerising. They did not seem to blink at all. The stare tore through his very core, chilling him to the bone. He wanted to cry. He wanted to go home.

He stood up. The cup rattled as he placed it back in the saucer.

"I've got to go now Dad, to get the last bus back to the station."

"Yeah, you do that. Tell your mother to come instead next time. We've got unfinished business to discuss."

CHAPTER 36 - JOSS

HE HAD TO sit down outside in the courtyard to recover. He let hot tears dry in his eyes as he gazed at the tinkling fountain and tried to regain some equilibrium. His phone started to vibrate inside the rucksack, and his fingers shook as he undid the zip to search for it. There were thirteen missed calls from his mother and one text from Tara:

'Ur mum's been phoning our house looking for u. My mum told her u weren't there before I could tell her not to say anything. Soz. x'

Christ!

"Hi Mum!" He tried to make his voice sound as normal as possible.

"Joss! Where are you? I've been trying to phone you." His mother sounded anxious.

"I'm in Norwich. Be home later."

"What are you doing?" "Hanging out with Benny."

"There's money missing from the cash box. Over a hundred pounds. Did you take it?" His mother's voice sounded as though she already believed he had.

"No. Of course not." The lie was instinctive and a weak attempt at self-preservation.

"I just know you're lying! Dad hasn't taken it and I certainly haven't. The money was for paying the gardener. Where is it Joss?" Her voice was rose in anger.

"I – I don't know! It wasn't me!"

"Come home now. If you're not home in half an hour there'll be trouble!"

His mother ended the phone call suddenly. Joss felt wretched and put his head in his hands. The day had started out so promising, but had begun to deteriorate as soon as he'd met his father. The man was clearly mad; dangerously insane. What was worse his dad now knew they lived in Norwich, close to the station. *Why ever hadn't he listened to his parents? It would take him at least another four hours to get home again. The shit would hit the fan as soon as he walked in the door.*

"All right, son?" The guard that Joss had spoken to earlier had a concerned look on his face.

"I'm okay. I'm going now."

He had a sudden frightening thought that halted him in his tracks.

"Will Edwin Evans be released soon, do you know?" The guard shrugged his shoulders.

"Patients are assessed regularly. If they are deemed fit to be released on licence, then they are moved to a halfway house that offers them support and help to readjust and fit back into the community. They are given a job of work to go to, and have to report to a probation officer once a week. Mr Evans will be released if it is appropriate."

He sounded as though he was reading from a textbook. Joss stood up and made his way to the exit. He wished the earth could swallow him whole. He could have bitten out his tongue at the thought of giving away the family's location.

He stepped through the half door and out onto the hospital driveway. Cars sped past on the main road in front of him, their owners oblivious to his plight. He crossed the road and waited for the bus back to East Croydon, the weight of the world on his shoulders. Only a few days' ago he'd had no worries other than being able to complete Loaf's essay on time.

While he waited he checked the train ticket was still in his pocket, and counted out the remaining money; nine pounds and fifty eight pence. *Just enough left to buy a sandwich, a bag of chips and a coke.*

How could he replace all the money in the cash box? As he sat on the bus he wracked his brain for an answer, but could find none. The deed was done; the money was spent. His phone vibrated several times in his pocket but he left it unanswered; there would be enough time to face up to his shortcomings later on.

The train back to London Bridge was surprisingly empty. Joss sat alone in the carriage apart from a business-type opposite him who was reading from an iPad. The man was dressed in an expensive-looking three-piece suit, and a briefcase rested on the floor by his feet. After a while the man fell fast asleep with his mouth open, the iPad still in his hands.

Acting on impulse and with a feeling of impending doom awaiting him on his return home, he put his rucksack quietly on his back and began to move the briefcase towards him gradually as the train slowed ready to pull into Manningtree station. The engines stopped and the man slept on. Joss snatched the briefcase, made his exit, and closed the door without a sound. Running the entire length of the platform he found an empty carriage at the back of the train. Heart racing with excitement, he opened the door, jumped in, and flung the briefcase on the seat as the train moved off towards Ipswich.

The case was locked. Searching in the zipped front pocket of his rucksack he found the small penknife he always kept there for emergencies. Jabbing frenziedly at the two locks he eventually prized them open.

The case was empty except for a large sealed envelope. Tearing it apart Joss found a pocket diary and a large amount of cash. Grinning from ear to ear he stuffed the envelope in his rucksack and hid the man's briefcase under one of the seats. When the train moved off from Ipswich station he saw the man's back as he walked towards the exit, and crouched down low in his seat. Checking that nobody else had got into the open carriage at Ipswich he had a quick count up of the money, and to his absolute delight he found there was a fifteen hundred pound stash in tens, twenties and fives.

He rested his head on the back of the seat and closed in eyes in relief. Everything would be alright now.

CHAPTER 37 - JOSS

HE TOOK A deep breath and turned his key in the lock. His parents came out at once into the hallway.

"I told you to come home ages ago! You're grounded, young man! This is way out of order!" His mother's face was livid-red with rage.

"Sorry Mum! I was in Norwich with Benny and we lost track of time. I was looking for something to buy Tara for her birthday." The lies slipped out easily, one after the other.

"The shops closed ages ago. Where have you been since then?" His father, unsmiling, came towards him as though looking him over for possible injuries.

"We went to the cinema. Sorry. I'm really sorry." Bowing his head, Joss actually did feel some sort of remorse for lying to his parents. However he couldn't bring himself to tell them the real reason for his absence.

"Where is the money that was in the cash box? You took it didn't you?" His mother always could see right through him. Joss reasoned it was futile to lie about that one.

"Yes I took it, but I couldn't find anything to buy Tara. It's still in my bag. I'll put it back in the cash box now. Sor-ry, but I really like her and wanted to buy her something." He sighed and looked down on the ground. He hoped his little-boy-lost look would work on his mother.

"You're grounded for a month! If you want money you're going to have to earn it like everybody else! You have to learn that you can't go stealing what's not yours. You can start tomorrow by washing the cars. There's plenty of other jobs around the house you can do as well."

"No Mum! Not for a month!"

"A month. I will be picking you up in the car as soon as school ends. Dad and I don't take kindly to being lied to or having our money stolen by our own son. One hundred pounds was to pay Bill. He came round this morning for his wages, and wasn't too pleased either when I couldn't pay him. You can pop over the road now, apologise, and give him his money!"

Shit!

With a heavy heart Joss swung his rucksack back over his shoulder, and with his parents watching his every move, he crossed the road and opened the gate to Bill's well-manicured garden. He fished around in his rucksack, retrieving £100 pounds from the envelope, and then knocked on the door. He shouted through the letterbox in case Bill had taken his hearing aid out.

"Bill, it's me; Joss!"

Joss could hear the sound of footsteps and then security chain being taken off. The old man put his head around the door.

"Hello Joss. This is a surprise! Come in." He opened the door further.

"No it's okay. I've just come to give you your wages. Sorry the money wasn't there earlier when you came round." He handed over the money, anxious to get away before the lonely old man started talking him to death.

"Thanks. Tell Mum I'll be over on Monday to prune the shrubs."

"Will do. Bye for now." Joss was already walking backwards down the path.

"All done." He brushed past his parents and headed for the stairs.

"Don't forget. You're grounded." He could feel his mother's eyes staring into his retreating back.

"How can I forget? You'll keep on reminding me!" He ran upstairs to his room and slammed the door.

He lay on his bed with the events of the day swimming around in his head. *Was he a bad lot just like his real dad?* He'd stolen his parents' money and the man's briefcase, but both crimes had been committed out of desperation. However, after seeing the disappointing reality that was his biological father, he now wished he'd listened to his mother and left well alone. *If only he was able to turn back the clock!*

'I'm grounded for a month. Will explain at school on Monday. x'

He'd just finished sending the text to Tara when there was a soft tapping on the door. Joss knew it wasn't his mother.

"Come in, Dad." He pushed his rucksack under the bed out of sight and lay back down on the pillow.

The door opened and the familiar face of the man he'd always thought was his father came into the room.

"Not a good day son, eh?" His father smiled at him in his usual charming way and came to sit down beside him on the bed.

"The worst. I'm sorry I took the money. At least I didn't spend it." He hoped his father would fall for the lie.

"Next time ask me. If only you'd asked me I could have given you an advance on your pocket money. There's no need to go stealing."

"I know. I will ask you next time. I really like Tara. I wanted to buy her something but got caught up with Benny and forgot."

"She's a nice girl."

"The best. I really like her, Dad." The *dad* came easily. Suddenly he wanted this man to think well of him. I'm not bad like my real father am I?" He sat up, confused and anxious.

"Of course you're not bad. You've just done something stupid today, and you'll learn from it. Take your punishment like a man and after a month we'll forget it ever happened."

If only his real dad could have been as kind!

"Sorry, Dad." Joss felt hot tears starting to fall. He wondered if he could live with himself for lying so glibly to his parents.

"Come here." His father held out his arms and Joss crawled into them, feeling loved, wanted, and safe.

CHAPTER 38 - JOSS

"WHY ARE YOU grounded?" Tara shared her apple with Joss as they sat on the wall outside the sixth form block.

"I wanted to see my dad, but didn't have any money for the train fare. I took the cash that Mum was going to use to pay our gardener with."

"You're in the shit then!" Tara laughed and shuffled closer. "Never mind. It's only for a month." She kissed him on the cheek, and Joss felt a stirring in his loins at her nearness.

"Why didn't you ask your parents for the money?" Tara thrummed her heels against the wall as she ate.

"They don't want me to visit him."

"Why not?"

"It's a long story; one that I don't really want to go into right now." Joss sighed with the weight of the secret he was carrying.

"You can tell me. I won't say anything."

Joss desperately wanted to unburden himself. He decided to take a chance on this girl he was liking more and more.

"He's a prisoner."

"He's in prison?" Tara looked at Joss, surprised.

"No, not the usual prison. It's like a secure hospital and he can't get out. He's mentally ill." He felt better straight away for telling her.

"Wow. No wonder they don't want you going there. He might be dangerous." Tara threw her apple core into a hedgerow and turned to look at Joss.

"He is dangerous, but I just wanted to meet him. I only found out about him recently. I never knew he existed." He closed his eyes with the relief of sharing his burden.

The bell rang for the end of morning break.

"Got to go or I'll be late for music theory. See you later." Tara jumped down from the wall, and Joss felt her warm hand on his.

"Text me any time. I won't tell a soul. Promise."

"I love you, Tara." His face felt hot with embarrassment.

"I love you too." She smiled at him and then was gone, mingling with the students going off to their various classrooms.

Joss sat stupefied for a few more minutes, amazed at Tara's revelation. Suddenly the world didn't seem such a bad place after all. Levering himself off the top of the wall he ran to catch his next class with a smile upon his face that refused to budge for the rest of the day.

True to her promise his mother was waiting for him in the car just outside the school gates. There was no chance for him to have another word with Tara. Joss opened the passenger door and got in.

"We're not going straight home." His mother looked grim. "We've got to visit the police station first. Dad's meeting us down there."

"Why?" He had a sudden frightening thought that his mother might be mad enough to report him.

"I had a visit from the police today. It seems that the money you gave Bill yesterday was counterfeit. Poor Bill got arrested trying to spend some of it in town this afternoon."

"What!" Joss could feel his heart start to race.

"Yes. When he was asked where he got the money from, Bill naturally told them we'd given it to him."

"Who's given it to us then? We don't know!" He began to panic.

"I withdrew the money from the bank on Friday. The money you gave Bill did not come from the bank. It had two watermarks on the paper instead of three. Where did it come from, Joss?" His mother started up the car and pulled away from the kerb, her lips set in a tight line.

Joss felt sick to his stomach. He had a sudden terrible thought of ending up a prisoner just like his real dad; rotten to the core. The bad genes had already been transferred from father to son; he would never be able to shake the legacy.

"It must have come from the bank! Where else would it have come from?" He tried one last time to absolve himself of any blame.

"We will get to the bottom of this at the police station. That's all I'm going to say just now."

The silence in the car was almost palpable. As they approached the station his mother found a space and parked the car. Joss looked out of the window and saw his father waiting for them at the main entrance, looking equally as grim.

But no, the man waiting for them was not his father; in fact he was not a blood relation at all. His real father was a kidnapper, rapist, and God knows what else!

CHAPTER 39 - JOSS

"JOSS, I'M DETECTIVE Inspector Mike Farrow. I expect you know why you're here with your parents today?"

Joss looked across the table to the burly dark-haired man sitting opposite, sipping coffee nonchalantly from a cracked mug.

"Yes. Mum told me." He tried to keep his voice from shaking with nervousness.

"What have you got to say about it all then?" The tone was even, and seemed to have a calming effect on his young interviewee.

"When I changed one of the twenty pound notes in a cafe I must have been given a dodgy tenner, that's all I can think of." Joss held his breath and prayed.

"It's a bit more than a dodgy tenner, son. When Mr Robertson gave us the rest of the money, the entire amount was counterfeit." Farrow put his cup down, and stared across the table.

Backed up into a corner like a trapped fox, Joss's heart started to race again. He looked at his parents sitting to his left but they were gazing at him incomprehensibly, waiting for an answer.

"I found it on a train."

"What train? Why were you on a train?" His mother sighed with exasperation.

"I didn't want to tell you. I went to see my dad."

"Good God!" His mother's face blanched under the fluorescent lighting.

"I knew you wouldn't like it, but I just had to see him. Now I wish I hadn't though." He bowed his head and looked at the floor.

"So this money was just sitting on a seat next to you, was it?" Skipping over the domestic issues, Farrow tried to keep the discussion on track.

"There was this rich-looking bloke opposite with a brief-case. When he fell asleep I took the briefcase to another carriage on the train and opened it. I was hoping there might be enough money in it to pay Mum and Dad back. That's all I wanted to do."

Joss felt relieved at the confession. He turned to his parents; his mother, sitting furthest away from him, briefly covered her face with her hands. He noticed his father placing an arm around his mother's shoulders.

"Joss, we've brought you up to know that stealing is wrong!"

"I know it is, Dad, but when Mum phoned to say the money was missing I knew I had to find a way to replace it!" To see his father so angry was upsetting Joss more than the police interview. He started to cry with the sure and certain knowledge that he'd let his parents down very badly.

Farrow rose from his chair.

"I'll organise some tea for you all and I'll be back in a moment." He turned and walked towards the door, closing it quietly behind him.

Joss let the tears fall freely.

"I'm bad like him! I'm no good! I'm going to be locked up!" He bent forward and sobbed loudly, unable to control his emotions.

His father shifted around in his seat and Joss felt an arm go across his back.

"You're not bad. Don't ever think that, eh? You've just not acted in the right way. We didn't realise how badly you needed to see your real dad. In a way some of this might possibly be our fault for not listening to you."

"He's mad! He frightened me!" Joss sobbed and wiped his eyes.

"I told you he was mad, you stupid boy!" His mother almost spat out the words. He had never seen her so angry.

"I-I'm s-so sorry!" Hiccupping, he took some deep breaths to try and regain his equilibrium. He felt his father's hand rubbing his back.

"Let this be a warning to you. You'll probably have a caution, but it's your first offence so it's highly unlikely you'll be locked up. Think hard and see if there's anything else you can help the police with, eh? It might stand you in good stead." His father's hands came back to rest in his lap.

When Farrow came back in the room with three cups of tea on a tray, Joss took the hot liquid gratefully.

"There's some sort of diary or address book in the envelope with the rest of the money." His voice was clear and concise, and Farrow pricked up his ears.

"Where's the envelope?"

"Under my bed."

"Was there anything else in the briefcase?" "No."

"I'll send a constable round and he can bring it back." Joss nodded, eager to make amends.

"Where were you travelling to?" Farrow chewed on some gum.

"I was coming home to Norwich. I'd been to Ardlington to see my dad." Joss made a point of not looking at his mother.

"Had you done this journey before?"

"No. It was the first time I'd ever seen my dad." "You've got to sixteen and never met your dad?" Farrow momentarily stopped chewing in surprise.

"He's in a secure hospital. Holmleas. Have you heard of it? My dad's Edwin Evans."

"Ah yeah, I know that place." Farrow seemed uncomfortable.

A silence settled over the room. Joss twisted his hands together backwards and forwards. He wanted to clear the slate once and for all.

"He said he'd be getting out. He said he'd be coming for my stepfather." Joss looked at his parents. His mother's face had frozen in terror.

"Idle threats. He won't be getting out of there in a hurry."

Farrow made a mental note to look back in the archives for anything relating to Edwin Evans, but first he had to put the teenager in front of him out of his misery.

"You're going to receive a caution this time Joss, as you've admitted your guilt and it's your first offence. The caution will stay on your record and you may have to disclose it if you apply for certain types of jobs later on in life. I expect you know quite well that you can't go around stealing money from your parents and stealing items that do not belong to you. Now we know of course why the owner of the briefcase did not report it stolen. Printing and distributing counterfeit money is a crime in itself, but hopefully we'll be able to see if there's anything in the address book that might help us catch the criminals. You'll need to give your details to the sergeant on the desk and be fingerprinted, but after that you're free to go."

As they made their way out of the station a short while later, Joss stayed close to his father.

"Can I ride back with you? I'm not Mum's favourite person at the moment."

"Yeah. Hop in."

Joss waved to his mother as she opened the driver door and sat down. There was no response.

"Be thankful you only got off with a caution, eh?"

"Perhaps the address book will be useful to them." Joss nodded to his father and gave a rueful smile. "I'm such a twat."

"No, you were entitled to see your real dad. You just went about it in the wrong way. If you want to see him again I'll drive you down there."

"You'd do that for me?" Joss looked up in surprise.

"Of course. Mum will have to get used to it. We can't stop you from seeing him."

Joss looked over as his father started up the engine.

"You're my real dad.   I don't want to see Evans again. There's something about him that gave me the creeps."

"I can't say I'm disappointed to hear that, because I'm not." Liam reached over and ruffled the top of his son's head.

"He wants Mum, and he wants you out of the way. As far as he's concerned I shouldn't have been born at all."

"He's a sick man. Hopefully he won't be getting out of there. Don't worry. You just think about your nice girl-friend. We've also got Easter coming up, and Amy and Toby will be here." Liam put the car in gear and pulled out of the car park.

"I think he'll get out. I think he'll be able to fool them that he's sane. You didn't see him, Dad. He's…..evil." Joss shivered, remembering the burning black eyes so much like his own. He wondered whether to tell his father that Evans now knew of their whereabouts, but at the last moment he decided to keep the information to himself.

"Don't worry Mum with any of this. She doesn't need to start thinking about Evans again. If you have any more con-cerns tell me, and we'll talk it over."

"Okay, Dad."

"Have a word with your mum when we get home. She's got a long list of jobs lined up for you to do to start paying off your debt."

Joss sighed as they joined the main road. An evening spent talking on the video phone to Tara and Benny now seemed rather less likely.

CHAPTER 40 - JOSS

PEERING UNOBTRUSIVELY THROUGH the net curtains covering the large bay window in the main living room, Joss looked on with envy as he saw his father and Toby step out of the Range Rover. His stepbrother was obviously his father's son, with the same soft Canadian accent and the same gentle laid-back air about him. After gathering copious amounts of luggage from the boot they made their way up the driveway to the front door, laughing and joking.

"Hey little brother! Good to see you!"

Joss stepped forward to receive a hug from the red-haired livewire whom he realised with a pang of regret was actually not his stepbrother at all.

"Hi Toby. Good flight?"

"Bearable. I spent 7 hours listening to some of Francois' new ideas for Kick & Scream songs. Some of them are awesome, but the majority suck!"

Although he was only 18 months older, Toby seemed so grown up. For the first time Joss felt a little in awe of the confident, strapping young man who stood in front of him.

"Hi Beth!" Toby gave his stepmother a bear-hug as she came out into the hallway to greet him.

"Toby, I swear you've grown another two inches! You're taller than your father now!" Beth extricated herself from Toby's vice-like grip, and held him at arm's length to look him over.

"You bet! I'm six feet four inches and ready to rock!"

Joss could see he only came up as far as Toby's shoulders. He reasoned with some dismay that he would probably have to spend his entire life looking up at his erstwhile stepbrother.

"You've got your usual room, Toby. I've put some towels in the en-suite for you." Beth smiled at her stepson's exuberance.

"Awesome. I'll have a shower now if that's ok? I could certainly do with one."

"Boy, you're sure full of energy!"

Joss felt another pang of envy as he noticed an affectionate expression on his father's face appear whilst watching his eldest son running up the stairs three at a time. Soon the sound of running water and Toby's melodic voice permeated into the rooms downstairs.

"Good to have him home, eh?"

Joss smiled at his father and mumbled something in agreement. *All it needed now was for his super-intelligent sister to come home at Easter, and then he could safely disappear into the background, unwanted and unexciting; a pain in the arse who should never have been born in the first place.*

He felt his phone vibrate; Tara was on the line. With some difficulty he ran up the stairs four at a time, opened the door to his bedroom, and accepted the call.

"How's it going, Joss?"

Hearing her voice made Joss want to reach out and touch her. He closed his door for privacy and flopped down on his bed.

"It's not. I'm still grounded for another two weeks, and to make it even worse the fucking rock god's turned up now."

"Who?"

"Toby; the groupie's delight. He lifts his little finger and all the girls come running, one after the other."

"Ah, Toby. He sounds dreamy. When can I meet him?" Tara laughed and pretended to swoon.

"Never, if I have anything to do with it. He's only here a week though. He'll piss off back home after Easter."

"It'll be ages now until we can meet up again." Tara sighed.

"Monday week at school. Life sucks. Are you going away for Easter?" Joss hoped Daniel Summerlee hadn't got his foot in the door.

"Nah. At home with the parents. How about you?"

"Grounded here with the parents, the rock god, and my sister." Joss stuck a finger down his throat and pretended to retch.

"Oh, you poor thing!" Tara's tinkly laugh echoed through the phone's speaker.

"And there's the big turkey dinner to get through yet as well."

"I'm sure you'll be able to manage that."

Joss heard a gentle knock on his bedroom door.

"Gotta go. Speak to you soon. Love you."

"Love you too." Tara blew him a kiss.

"Who's there?" Joss sat up and put his phone back in his pocket.

The handle turned and Toby's lanky frame filled the doorway. Freshly showered and wearing a clean pair of jeans and a t-shirt, he ran his fingers through his damp hair and grinned.

"Hey, little brother! Are there any good nightclubs around here?" He came and plonked himself down on the bed, much to Joss's irritation.

"Yeah, in Norwich, but you'll have to go on your own or with Amy; I'm grounded."

"I heard about that. Dad was telling me on the way back from the airport."

"Great. What else was he telling you?"

"Only that you didn't come home on time and went to see your dad without telling them."

"Yeah, well. I'd only just found out about him." Joss felt somewhat relieved that his father hadn't mentioned the counterfeit money episode.

"I'd have gone there too if it were me. Amy and I had been sworn to secrecy since we were kids. We were told never to mention your dad to you at all."

"Well, now you can because I've found out about him. What a prick he is as well. You don't know how lucky you are, having a dad that's normal." Joss felt another stab of envy go through him, and he kept his gaze down on the carpet.

"At least you get to live with my dad. I've grown up without him mostly." Toby sighed and looked serious for a moment. "As a kid I'd have given anything to live here with him."

"Really?" Joss looked up, surprised.

"Yeah. All my friends had dads except me. Mine was always three thousand miles away."

"What about Mike?"

"What about him?"

"Don't you get on?"

"I gave him a hard time, growing up. He wasn't my dad and I never got the feeling that he actually liked me. Then Mom had Trisha and I always felt left out."

Joss looked at his stepbrother and suddenly saw a kindred spirit.

"Jeez. Are we fucked up or what?"

"You bet your sweet ass, little brother. Well and truly fucked up."

"I bet I'm more fucked up than you are."

"Yeah. What a little fucker!"

They looked at each other, and Joss threw a pillow. Toby ducked, caught it, and took a well-aimed return shot, hitting Joss square in the face. They both laughed, and suddenly Joss had the feeling that perhaps the following week would not be so hard to endure after all.

CHAPTER 41 - JOSS

"AMY'S SENT A text to say her train will arrive at Norwich in half an hour. Do you two want to come with me to meet her?"

Joss looked up from trying to get his fingers in the right position on Toby's guitar to make a decent C chord.

"I'm grounded, Dad. Don't you remember?"

"I'll make an exception for your sister's sake."

"Okay. Can we go bowling afterwards?"

"Now you're extracting the urine."

"I'll go." Toby took the guitar from Joss and gave him a playful punch. "Come on little brother, it's time to meet the brains of the family."

"Yeah, well it's certainly not me. I'm the twat of the year." Joss whispered behind his father's back and gave Toby a return punch.

Liam pulled up in front of the station just as the train arrived. Amy greeted them all with a flurry of kisses and a waft of expensive perfume.

"Dad! So lovely to see you!" She threw her arms around her father's neck.

"We've missed you so much!" Liam smiled as he did a quick double-take; incredulous at Amy's resemblance to her mother.

"When is it my turn?" Toby laughed and looked at his stepsister fondly.

"Right now!" Amy gave him a hug and then turned her attention to Joss, who tried unsuccessfully to dodge the kiss that was coming his way.

"My, my! Every time I see you you've grown a little bit more!"

"You should know why, doctor!" Joss, embarrassed and undemonstrative by nature, found himself blushing.

"Not yet; still a student. Another year to go." Amy pulled the corners of her mouth downwards and grimaced.

"You'll get there; you've got enough brains for all of us." Joss looked at his beautiful sister with her long blonde hair flying in the stiff March breeze, and felt yet another wave of jealousy overcome him.

"Come on. Mom's got some lunch ready." Liam stowed his daughter's bags in the back of the Range Rover, and started up the engine.

"How's the band going, Toby?" Amy turned around in the front seat and looked over her shoulder, as Liam manoeuvred the car out of the approach to the station.

"Great. We're signed now and getting a lot of interest; got some festivals to play in the summer, and a couple of arena gigs supporting some big bands. I might even be earning enough from it soon to be able to afford to leave home. I'm sure Mike's looking forward to that!" Toby grinned and caught his father's eye winking in the rear view mirror.

"My girlfriend's even heard of Kick and Scream, so you must be doing well." Joss wondered if he would ever match up to his sister and brother.

"You've got a girlfriend? You must be growing up at last!" Amy laughed and turned towards Joss.

"Yeah. Her name's Tara. She's cool."

"I'd like to meet her."

"You will at Christmas. I'm grounded. She's not al-lowed round at the moment."

"Yes, I heard about that." Amy looked at her father, who maintained a tactful silence.

"Glad to be able to keep the family entertained." Joss fought down a wave of irritation.

"Mum and I have to find something to talk about on the phone. My life's boring at the moment; all study and nothing else. You're the one doing all the exciting things."

"Yeah. Welcome to my world. It's a laugh a minute."

With the short journey home completed, Joss stepped out of the Range Rover as his mother opened the front door.

"Amy! So lovely to see you! Now I've got all my family around me!"

Joss watched the two women embracing, and felt the special bond between them; such a close bond that he would never be a part of. He felt apart from all of them; there was not only his darker colouring to contend with, but also his growing disinterest in academia. He somehow felt drawn to practical skills. He was beginning to enjoy his woodwork lessons, and by his own admission had made more than a passable effort in building a bird table for his mother's forthcoming birthday. His teacher was pleased, and he hoped his mother would be also. He felt adrift in a sea of finely-tuned intelligent brainpower, but wanted desperately to fit in and be something other than a disappointment to his family.

EASTER 2012

CHAPTER 42

"TIME TO CARVE, Dad!"

Joss carried the steaming roasted turkey into the dining room on a stainless steel platter, and watched his father as he heaped thick, succulent slices of white meat onto the best china plates that only ever seemed to come out at Easter and Christmas.

"Thanks, Beth. This is superb!"

Toby gave an appreciative eye to the fare on offer, and helped himself to a selection of vegetables.

"Well, it is Easter Sunday, and it's not every day the family is together. Let's make the most of it." Beth smiled as she passed the gravy boat around.

"It's a shame Paul's working over Easter. He would have loved to have been here today." Amy poured gravy into the middle of her Yorkshire pudding. "He volunteered to work the extra shifts at double time to get the rest of the deposit. We're only five thousand pounds short now, but after that we've got to start saving for the wedding."

"Have you started house-hunting?" Liam took the gravy boat from his daughter.

"Not yet, but we will soon. We want to be near both sides of the family, so we'll probably be looking around the Bury area, as Paul's family lives in Ipswich. We've researched Bury on the Internet, and it looks really nice."

"Has it got an arena? I'll bring the band over to play." Toby laughed and took another slice of turkey.

"Yes, a small one I think. It's called The Apex, but I'm not sure if it'll be suitable for Francois. He growls too much. Listening to that file you sent me, he sounds like a creature from the deep with a chronic case of laryngitis."

"It's paying the bills though. The creature sent me a text this morning. We've been asked to play at your Download festival in June. I'll be able to get out from under Mike's feet after that. What do you think of that, eh?"

"Wow! Can you get me a guest pass?" Joss had stopped chewing in surprise.

"Sure can, little brother, if you're not still grounded! There'll be passes for all of you."

"Does that mean I'll have to mingle with the great un-washed, all wearing offensive t-shirts?" Amy wrinkled her nose in disgust.

"Sure does. I'll even lend you one of mine."

Listening to the good-humoured banter all around him, Joss yearned to be able to impart some good news of his own. However, he could think of nothing worthwhile to say. The talking went on all around him, and he remained silent.

"You're quiet, Joss." His mother put down her knife and fork, took a sip of wine, and looked at her son.

"He's missing his girlfriend." Amy laughed. "He's in love."

"Shut up, Amy." Joss felt himself blushing with embarrassment.

"Aw, let the poor guy see his girl, eh?" Toby's eyes twinkled with amusement.

"What about it Beth?" Liam poured himself some more wine. "It is Easter after all."

Joss looked at his mother hopefully.

"Okay. She can join us for tea today if you like." Beth sighed; outvoted.

"Great! Thanks Mum!" Joss reached for the phone in his pocket, as Toby and Amy clapped and cheered.

"After dinner with the phone calls, please."

His mother fixed him with one of her stares. Joss let the phone slide back in his pocket and willed the dinner to be over with as quickly as possible.

"What's your best subject at school these days?"

Joss looked up from his plate towards his sister. He knew the answer to that one.

"Woodwork. I like making things with my hands. I think I want to be something like a builder or a carpenter when I leave school."

"Makes a change from going to medical school." Amy smiled at her brother.

"No. Don't want to do that. I'd be no good at it." "Each to his own, eh?" Toby helped himself to the leftover vegetables. "I couldn't decide what I wanted to do for years, but I knew it had to be something to do with music.

Mom let me do the sound engineering course at college, and the rest is history, so they say."

"I can only make things. I can't play any instruments or cure sick people. I'm thick." Joss mumbled into his food.

"Don't ever say that, Joss. You're not thick at all. You just have different skills to your brother and sister, eh?" Liam laid down his knife and fork and wiped his mouth with a serviette.

Joss had a burning question in his head that would not go away, no matter how hard he tried. Whilst his mother and Toby were in the kitchen seeing to the dessert, Joss decided to broach the subject.

"Dad; do you know what my real father did for a living before he was locked up?"

He heard Amy take in a quick breath.

"Joss, Mum doesn't want to hear about him. I'm not sure I do either."

"Sorry Amy, but I need to know." Joss hoped his mother would not make an entrance too soon.

"It's okay. Of course you want to know. For your information, he was self-employed; a builder and architect I believe."

Liam stated the answer matter-of-factly in an even tone, dissipating the sudden tension that had built up in the room.

"Thanks, Dad."

"Any time you have a question, just ask me. I'll do my best to answer."

However, unfortunately as far as Joss was concerned, his father's reply further convinced him that he was somehow different from his family. He shared no common interests with any of them, and nobody in the family seemed to be of a practical nature. He thought back and remembered how his father had recently paid out a small fortune for a new kitchen to be fitted.

His real father would have known how to fit it himself!

NOVEMBER 2012

CHAPTER 43 – EDWIN

EDWIN EVANS SAT on his favourite seat in the courtyard, immune to the cold November wind. He watched the fish swimming around and around in the small pond, and likened himself to a fish; the walls of the pond were like the walls of the hospital. He could not escape, and neither could the fish; in fact they were worse. If they managed to escape from the pond they would still not be able to break free from the confines of the hospital; unwitting inhabitants of a prison within a prison.

The little orange bodies were mesmerising him; swimming to and fro, to and fro. He failed to even notice the warden patrolling the courtyard until he sat down right next to him.

"Hey, Edwin! Do you want the good news or the bad news?" Ben Hawkes' usual stern countenance broke out into a rare smile.

Edwin looked up with irritation. Somebody else was sitting on *his* seat.

"Neither. I just want to be left alone." He turned his gaze back to the pond.

"Well I'll tell you anyway."

"Fuck off."

Hawkes persevered.

"The bad news is that you won't be able to eat hospital food for much longer. Don't you want to know why?"

Hawkes' conversation suddenly registered in Edwin's brain. He turned around on his seat to face the warden with an inquisitive look on his face.

"What the fuck are you talking about?" He sighed and felt like punching the man's lights out.

"What I'm saying is that your latest interview went well. The good news is they're talking about giving you a trial out on licence in Braemar House. What do you say?"

At first the enormity of Hawkes' words failed to register with their recipient. However, after a minute or so a slow grin spread across Edwin's lined features.

"They're letting me out?"   He could hardly believe his ears.

"Not fully, no. You'll be given a furnished flat within the complex and supervised, but you'll be allowed out locally to go to work and to buy food. If you behave yourself at Braemar and show you can hold down a job, after six months you can move on and rent a place of your own. You'll just need to report to a social worker once a week."

"Jesus Christ! Cheers for that Benny!" Edwin shook the warden's hand.

Edwin got up from his seat, and felt like dancing around the pond. The fish looked up at him with hopeful eyes. He threw in some pellets of food from a wooden box nailed to the courtyard wall, gazed up at the sky, and laughed out loud.

"I'm getting out!"

Hawkes observed the man he had watched over for nearly 17 years. *He was now either completely sane and ready to take his place in society, or was still as mad as a hatter and had fooled them all.*

"Don't forget, you'll be closely supervised for six months."

"Yeah, yeah, so what's new? When will I be going then?"

"Next week; probably Monday morning. Good luck to you, Edwin."

"Cheers."

As Hawkes continued patrolling the courtyard, he could not help but have a little niggling doubt as to whether the decision of the powers-that-be to let Edwin leave the safety of the hospital was actually the correct one, or whether the repercussions would come back to haunt them in the future. Only time would tell.

Back in his room, Edwin looked around the familiar surroundings that had been his home for so long. There wasn't much to pack as far as he could see; a few clothes, some toiletries, some paperbacks, and the framed photographs of his mother and father they'd let him keep. *Not much to show for a life lived for nearly 60 years.*

He thought back to what he'd had before it all went wrong; the house, the car, the business, his daughter, but most of all…Beth. *That little shit had taken the whole lot away from him by being born, and he'd even had the nerve to come and visit!*

Edwin punched the wall with his fist, feeling the tension leave his body.

His son would be the first one to pay. He would wait until the time was right, bide his time, keep his nose clean, and then claim Beth back, who had been rightfully his in the first place. That little fucker had only been good for one thing; he'd bleated on about living in Nor-wich close to the station. Sooner or later one of them would be getting off the train...................

She had been the girl of his dreams; he had had her all to himself for ten years. The fuckers who had kicked him senseless at school would have liked to own a woman like Beth. He, Edwin, had owned her body and soul before it had all gone wrong and he had been put into this shithole of a place.

He hated the constant sounds of other people. At home he had had the choice of whether to go downstairs and see Beth or stay upstairs by himself. It suited him fine, but now the voices of madmen were all around him; at times it seemed as if their senseless noise was trying to take over his brain.

Sometimes he yearned to go back to his childhood, even though he had spent a good part of it locked in the cupboard under the stairs. However, it had been quiet and peaceful in the cupboard. After his mother had turned the key she would stop shouting and stagger off to do more drinking. It became a bizarre refuge when his father had died and his mother had been unable to cope; there were no noises and no voices, and he could do what he liked in his little home. As he became older he could read in peace under the single lightbulb dangling from the staircase; books on architecture and the built environment that he had managed to filch from the library when he had to go out and buy her more alcohol.

He missed his father. One day he had been there, and the next day he was gone. Pouf.... in a puff of smoke. They had told him it was a bleed into the brain or something like that. All he knew was that his life was never the same after the night he had got up to go to the toilet and saw his father lying dead on the bathroom floor. He remembered how he had pissed himself there and then in fright; his voice seeming to come from a long way off as he screamed. He had been seven years old. His father had been the centre of his universe. In times to come he often wished his mother had died instead.

Nobody ever questioned why he was not attending school on a regular basis. If it had not been for the library books which he had read over and over again and the evening classes he had taken as a teenager when he had been strong enough to break free, he would never have been able to earn a decent living.

He had found her dead that morning of his exam. He had felt no emotion at the sight of her lying on her back having choked on her own vomit. He remembered going off to college, taking the exam, and then coming back to phone for an ambulance. He knew it was too late; she was already purple and stiff as a board, but he had to go through the motions.

He smiled at how his life had taken an upward turn after the funeral. He had passed the exam to become an apprentice builder. He had tidied up the house that his mother had sullied with her filth and bottles of vodka. He always liked sitting alone in the cellar; in fact he had liked it so much that when he had finally earned good money he extended it himself, even putting in that toilet so he didn't have to trudge upstairs if he was taken short.

Yeah, life had been good until the childhood flashbacks started and he found he needed something to dull the reality and make him comfortably numb. At first smoking weed helped, but later, after the rush of cocaine, he failed to realise he had inherited his mother's addictive nature until it was too late. With superhuman effort he had managed to chase the dragon into hell while Beth had been with him, but now he needed her back in her rightful home just in case the craving took him over once more.......

CHAPTER 44 - EDWIN

THE WORK WAS tedious. However, Edwin was nothing if not a perfectionist. He stacked the supermarket shelves with a military precision; the label of each tin always faced the same way, and was lined up perfectly with the one next to it. He was well aware that he had become an object of ridicule amongst his teenage co-workers, but he kept himself to himself and made sure his anger never bubbled to the surface, especially when some stupid customer would take a tin from his carefully constructed pile and throw it in carelessly in their trolley.

He made himself popular with the management. He was always early for his shift, and always let it be known that he did not mind staying over time to help out with work in other departments. After his three-month trial he was promoted to assisting the manager in charge of the grocery department; making sure every fruit and vegetable compartment was always well-stocked with produce from the warehouse, and answering customer enquiries. The work was still tedious, but the managers were pleased with Edwin's diligence.

At the end of his shift Edwin would walk the two miles home to his little four-roomed flat in Braemar House. He saved his wages, kept himself apart from the other inhabitants, and made sure he was always on time for the daily meetings with his social worker. If he was not needed to work a weekend shift he would spend his time in the local Internet café, trawling through estate agents' websites looking for a suitable place to rent; near enough to get to Norwich on the train, but far enough away not to cause any suspicion.

Before he knew it the two mile walk home was being taken under a summer sky and with the birds still twittering in the trees. Edwin was pleased; the physical work in the supermarket had made him fitter than he'd been in years, he had some money in his post office account, and things were indeed looking up.

One day in the middle of a heatwave he arrived back home to find a note from Danny, the Social Worker, pinned to his front door to say he would be calling again that evening. Edwin *tutted* with annoyance, and tore the note into shreds. He was just finishing his meal of roast chicken, chips and peas, when he heard the inevitable knock on the door.

"Hello Edwin; may I come in?"

"Sure Danny. I was just finishing my dinner."

"Had a good day at work?"

"Not too bad. There's talk of me being promoted again. Nothing definite, but I'm keeping my fingers crossed."

Danny nodded sagely.

"I've only been hearing good things about you, Edwin."

"Well, I've tried hard to keep in their good books. It looks as if it might be paying off at last."

"Indeed. Indeed." Danny Vincent looked at the man standing in front of him and wondered what it was about

Edwin that always made him feel edgy. He couldn't put his finger on quite what it was, but there was definitely something about the man that just did not gel right with him. "It looks as though you'll be able to move off from Braemar House quite soon. You're holding down your job, and if you're agreeable you can start looking for somewhere of your own to rent now." Danny smiled with his mouth, but his eyes stayed focused.

"Great. I was thinking somewhere like Colchester. My cousin lives near the town centre there."

"Ok. I'll inform Essex social services, but you'll only need to report in once a week now to their office. Ask the HR department at the supermarket for help in transferring you to their branch in Colchester. They'll be able to give you a good reference."

"Will do."

Danny felt relieved to be able to escape out of the front door. At the last moment he realised what he found disconcerting about the man; it was the eyes. *Edwin's voice was soft, but the black, beady eyes were mesmerising.* He would have to make enquiries as to the whereabouts of Evans' victims. They would need to know he was out on his own.

CHAPTER 45 - EDWIN

EDWIN LEFT BRAEMAR house at the end of July without so much as a backward glance, and found a one bedroom flat to rent in Colchester about a 20 minute walk from the train station. He remembered that his cousin probably lived nearby, but did not have any burning desire to find out for certain. He took his prescribed medications on time, reported to his new social worker once a week, cooked a meal for one each evening, and kept his new flat clean and tidy.

The reference from his previous employer stood him in good stead, and within a short time had been promoted to the post of produce manager at the Colchester branch. He ran his team with military precision, but spoke to nobody unless it was to do with work issues. He was aware the staff laughed at him behind his back and thought him odd, but his team were somehow mindful to arrive punctually for their shifts and to wear a smartly pressed uniform and a willing smile. Customers often commented on how tidily and neatly the vegetables were stacked in their little plastic compartments.

Edwin waited, and then waited some more. When his social worker only needed to see him once a month, he began to formulate some plans. The freedom from interfering busybodies gave him the chance to catch the train unobserved and make some forays into Norwich on his days off. He found a seat outside the station where he could sit and watch the people coming and going. He would be nearer to her there; he felt he could almost reach out and touch her hair.

He had all the time in the world. The weather was good, and not a soul noticed him sitting there hour after hour. People rushed by him, busy with their own lives. He scanned the faces of the women going in and out of the station, and knew that if he was patient one day he would catch a glimpse of her.

When the weather started to change he wrapped up warmly and brought flasks of hot soup with him on the train. The afternoon sun set too soon in the run-up to Christmas, and Edwin had to catch an earlier train home than usual when it became too dark to see people's faces.

Then on the last Saturday afternoon before Christmas just as he had decided to go back, he saw her coming out of the station. She was laughing and holding hands with a man dressed in jeans and a long black overcoat, who carried a large holdall. Her long blonde hair was flying in the wind, and her head was close together with his as they shared some private joke that he would never be a part of. At one point they stopped to kiss, and Edwin felt the anger start to rise

Putting his rucksack on his back he followed at a discreet distance as they turned right out of the station and hurried along the road. It had started to rain slightly, and he saw the man put an umbrella over Beth's hair. They cuddled closer to keep out of the rain. Edwin's hands scrunched into fists as he walked, the knuckles white in his pockets.

Within about 10 minutes they opened a garden gate and walked up the path to a detached double-fronted house. Edwin made a mental note of the number of the house and the name of the road. With the hood to his jacket pulled well down over his head he walked on by, and saw a middle-aged woman open the front door and let the couple in. His last vision was of the outside light picking out glints of gold in Beth's hair as she embraced the older woman and stepped inside the house with the man.

Edwin thought long and hard on the train ride home. He would have to see his social worker the following day, but then the supermarket would be closed for Christmas for a couple of days. The festive season stretched out empty before him. He had all the time in the world to plan just exactly how he was going to get Beth back again. She had been taken so rudely from him all those years ago, but now he could finally see the light at the end of the tunnel, and once he had her he would never let her go again.

CHAPTER 46 - JOSS

"AW MUM, YOU'RE not bringing out those terrible decorations again that I made at primary school are you?"

Joss complained good-naturedly as his mother prepared to tie a paper bauble onto the Christmas tree that had been haphazardly coloured in many years before with a child's red crayon.

"Of course! Why wouldn't I?" Beth laughed. "This is very precious to me. You've written 'I love my mummy' on it."

"Oh God." Joss hid his head under a cushion.

"I think it's lovely." Tara brought out another one from the box. "This one just says 'Jos' with one s."

"It took him years to be able to spell Jocelyn."

"I am here you know." A muffled voice spoke from beneath the cushion.

"Come out you wimp. Mum will be bringing my ones out in a minute." Amy plonked herself down on the sofa next to Joss. "I'll never understand why we have to put a tree in our front room just because it's Christmas."

"Prince Albert started it back in the 1850's I think. Blame him. Paul, here's some of Amy's." Beth held up a wonky-looking angel with a broken halo.

"Was she drunk at the time?" Paul laughed as he unravelled a string of coloured lights.

"I was only eleven, so I don't think so. It was my first proper Christmas." Amy was pensive and suddenly uncharacteristically quiet.

"Don't dwell on the past darling, just enjoy the present." Beth smiled. "We're going to have a lovely time over the next few days."

"But don't you ever think of it; of him?" Amy stood up to help her mother decorate the tree.

"No. I try not to. It's all in the past now. It'll do us no good to keep thinking about it."

Beth was glad she had kept it to herself when told that Evans had been released. What Amy and the family didn't know, they didn't need to worry about.

"How's it going in here? Liam came into the room carrying an aluminium ladder from the garage, with Toby following behind. "Come on Joss, you can help out eh? Can you hand me up some of those ceiling decorations? Hold the ladder steady, Toby." Liam climbed up the ladder holding a large silver bell.

"Can't I just sit here and watch?" Joss sighed and stuffed a warm mince pie in his mouth.

"It's ok, I'll help you." Tara stuck her tongue out at Joss and handed Liam up a glittering 'Merry Christmas' sign.

"Thank you Tara. It's a good thing someone wants to help."

"I'm eating." Joss took another mince pie and remained seated.

Beth looped fairy lights around the tree and switched them on, hoping against hope that they still worked after a year packed away in the loft. A cheer went up around the room as the bulbs sprang to life.

"Who's going to midnight mass tonight?" She stood back to admire her handiwork.

"We're all going aren't we?" Amy looked at Paul, who nodded.

"Of course. It's a Darrah family tradition!" Liam stepped down from the ladder. "Ok with you Toby?"

"Sure. Mom and Mike usually go. Christmas Eve wouldn't be the same without midnight mass."

"I'll do dinner for eight o'clock then. Pork and apple sauce, roast potatoes, and vegetables. Volunteers needed to help set up and clear away."

"Joss and I will help, Beth." Tara sat down next to Joss and gave him a kiss.

"Did my lips move? Did I agree to this?" Joss chewed on a third mince pie.

"Yep!" Tara and Beth both spoke in unison.

CHAPTER 47 - EDWIN

A LIGHT BLANKET of snow lay undisturbed on the quiet road. Edwin shivered inside his black duffel coat and pulled the hood well over his head as he walked towards the house on the opposite side of the road. He could see a light on in the porch, but otherwise the rest of the rooms were in total darkness.

Crossing over the road he opened the garden gate quietly and tiptoed unnoticed around to the back of the house, where he found that thankfully several large leylandii offered him good cover.

Switching on his torch, he tried the patio doors but found them locked. He then tried the handle of the double-glazed kitchen door, but it did not budge. Moving along past the kitchen there was a door to some kind of outbuilding. Edwin pulled the handle down and was surprised when it yielded. He opened the door and found himself inside a gar-age-cum-workshop.

Flashing his torch around the inside of the garage he could see the outline of the family car; *one of those flashy Range*

Rover jobs. Ladders and tools were hung on hooks on the walls, and he could see some old tins of paint and used paintbrushes on a long workbench that ran along the left side.

Moving past the car towards the front of the garage he came across a door on the right hand side of the wall. Somebody had left a ladder propped up next to the door, which somehow looked out of place. Shining his torch on the handle, he turned it and found himself inside the house near to main entrance. He could see the light in the porch shining through the half-glazed inner front door.

There were no sounds of life in the house at all. Looking about him, he could see a white burglar alarm sensor in a corner above the inner door. He noticed there was no usual red light flashing indicating that it had been turned on, and Edwin decided to take a chance.

Keeping away from any likely pressure pads near the front door or at the foot of the stairs just in case, he crept onto the first step and inched his way upwards towards the bedrooms. He could hear nothing apart from clocks ticking away the moments until his hated and lonely Christmas Day. He stepped over another likely pressure pad at the top of the stairs, and had another look around.

Five doors were open along the landing, and another one right at the end was closed. Creeping on tiptoe Edwin looked in the first one; a bedroom with a double bed in it and various items of men's clothing scattered on the duvet, probably pulled out of the suitcase he could see lying on the floor. There was a guitar by the bed on a stand.

He moved along to the room next to it; a boy's room judging by the posters on the walls and the masculine décor. *His son's room! The little shit whose fault it had all been in the first place!* There was no sign of the boy. Edwin's sense of orderliness baulked at the sight before him; the unmade bed, the dirty cup and plate on the bedside table, and the possessions strewn haphazardly about the room.

The room next to the boy's room was a bathroom and toilet. Edwin noticed how clean the room was, and how the matching pink towels and flannels were the same colour as the soap and the shower curtain. *Did she use this room? Was that her perfume in the air?* He became aroused, imagining her soaping her naked body. He had to turn away as his mind started to wander from its goal.

His goal! Walking confidently along the upstairs landing, now certain that the house was temporarily unoccupied, Edwin investigated the next two bedrooms at his leisure. They were definitely occupied by females; the rooms both had en-suite bathrooms, large double beds, and were fluffy, frilly and flouncy. He opened drawers and cupboards, fingering lacy panties, slips and brassieres. He felt a rage starting deep within him at the sight of men's clothing hanging up on one side of both built-in wardrobes, and he had to sit down on one of the beds and take a deep calming breath as he had been taught to do years before at the hospital.

He opened the door to the last bedroom, which he decided was obviously a spare single room as all it contained were a bare mattress and empty cupboards and shelves. Edwin grinned to himself; it would be a perfect place to wait until the family were settled and asleep. Nobody would think of going in there, and there was even a comfortable-looking armchair next to the bed for him to sit in.

But first his bladder needed emptying; there could be a long wait until the family returned. Edwin went into the bathroom, turned on the light, lifted up the toilet seat, and relieved himself. He flushed the toilet, lowered the lid, and washed his hands at the sink. Before he went back to the spare room he straightened the mat around the toilet, wiped the sink, and lined up the towels neatly side by side, He folded the flannel and placed it next to the soap, turning off the light as he went out.

His rucksack was heavy on his back. He went back into the spare bedroom, closed the door again and unbuckled the rucksack; sighing with relief. He took off his duffel coat and sank into the armchair, undoing the zip of his rucksack and taking out a round of ham and tomato sandwiches and a bottle of water. After he had eaten he packed any rubbish back in his rucksack, making sure the knife in its leather sheath was within easy reach. Then he turned off his torch, sat in the dark, and waited.

CHAPTER 48

"ALL THAT SINGING'S made me thirsty!" Amy took off her gloves and scarf and hung her coat up on one of the hooks in the hallway.

"Hot chocolate before bed anyone?" Beth smiled and looked around at her brood.

"Yes please." Toby and Liam spoke almost simultaneously.

"I will. How about you, Paul?" Amy looked towards her fiancée.

"Sure. Thanks, Beth." Paul ran his hands over Amy's smooth blonde locks and gave her a kiss. "Happy birthday sweetheart; did you think I wouldn't remember?"

"I knew you would!" Amy gave him a hug.

"I'll say goodnight and go on up. I want to phone Tara. Merry Christmas everyone! Happy birthday Amy!" Joss threw his jacket on the floor and bounded up the stairs.

"Merry Christmas little brother!" Toby's distinctive tones echoed up onto the landing above.

Joss closed his bedroom door and quickly changed into a t-shirt and shorts. Pulling the duvet around him he picked up his mobile phone, found Tara's number and pressed the call button.

"That's quick; I've only just got in!" Tara gave a chuckle.

"I just wanted to make sure you and your mum got home okay." Joss spoke in uncharacteristically soft tones.

"Of course we did; it's only round the corner!"

"Well, you never know who's about do you?"

"Don't be such a twat."

"Alright. Merry Christmas Tara: Love you loads." "Love you too. It's going to be a great Christmas. I'll see you tomorrow – oh no, wait. See you later on today!"

"Yeah, night night babe."

"Night night."

Joss switched the phone onto vibrate mode, and put it in its usual place under his pillow, just in case Tara woke up and sent him a message during the night. He lay back on the pillow and closed his eyes. He heard the rest of the family coming upstairs, followed by the familiar sound of water running in Amy and Paul's en-suite shower. Over this he could distinctly hear Toby playing a few chords on his guitar. He felt safe and happy, surrounded by his loving family. He thought ahead to his 18th birthday coming up after Christmas. He fell asleep in no time at all with a small smile playing about his lips.

Amy dried herself, cleaned her teeth, and rubbed aqueous cream into her skin.

"I should be doing that!" Paul laughed from the depths of the shower.

"Too late, mate. I've already done it." She brushed her hair and stepped into her nightdress.

"I won't be long. Warm up the bed for me, 'cos I'm coming to get ya!" Paul turned off the water and emerged dripping from the shower.

"This is my parents' house. No hanky panky. They're just next door. It'll be too embarrassing." Amy chuckled as she climbed underneath the duvet.

"Not even a little bit?" Paul swung the towel over his head and dried his back in a vigorous side-to-side motion, thrusting out his hips and making his penis swing back and forth.

"Will you stop it! No; they can probably hear every word you're saying!" Amy reached out to try and grab the undulating member, but Paul jumped backwards out of reach just in time.

"Looks like I'm going to have to tie a knot in it then."

"I can do that for you."

"Bugger off." Paul found some pyjama bottoms in his suitcase and snuggled into bed beside Amy and turned off the light.

"Give us a kiss then, if nothing else."

"Alright." Amy pursed her lips but then opened her mouth to receive Paul's tongue.

"Love you. And happy birthday again darling. I've got a blinder of a present for you later on."

"Love you too. I can't wait!"

"I can't wait for some hanky panky." He pulled Amy's head onto his chest and closed his eyes, enjoying the feel of her body close to his.

"Did you put the burglar alarm on?" Beth sat up in bed at the sudden thought.

"No, I forgot. I've got a feeling I didn't lock the door to the garage either. Did you?" Liam was already getting out of bed again and putting on his dressing gown as he spoke.

"I didn't know it was unlocked in the first place."

"I opened it to get a ladder out of the garage earlier on. I'll go and check now." He opened the bedroom door and went downstairs, returning after a few moments.

"All locked and bolted. No-one's getting in here to-night."

"Glad to hear it." Beth turned on her right side, enjoying the feel of Liam's warm arms encircling her. "Did you leave the landing light on? Amy still doesn't like the dark."

"Yes I remembered that. Goodnight darling. Merry Christmas." Liam kissed the back of her neck. "Shall we give Amy her birthday present at dinner tonight?"

"Yes, lovely. She'll be so excited! Goodnight."

CHAPTER 49 - EDWIN

HE SWITCHED ON the torch and looked at his watch; the hands showed twenty five minutes to three.

Time to claim what was rightfully his!

Edwin stood up from the armchair, slightly stiff after having sat for so long. He put his duffel coat on and buckled the rucksack to his back, after taking out the knife and putting it into his pocket.

Treading carefully in case there were any loose floorboards, he quietly opened the door of the spare room and crept out onto the landing. All the bedrooms had their doors closed, but he knew she would not be in either of the two rooms at the far end.

Quietly turning the handle of the door nearest to him the dimmed landing light picked out the faces of a slumbering middle-aged couple, both with short grey hair. Edwin closed the door again noiselessly and felt a wave of irritation wash over him. *She just had to be in the next room!*

When he eased open the next door along, he had to stand still for a moment and take some deep calming breaths.

The woman that had never left his thoughts for even a minute all the time he was in hospital lay before him in the bed, her long blonde hair spread out all over her pillow. In the place where he should have been lay a man, bare-chested and with his right arm around Beth's shoulder. He saw Beth's head on the man's chest and all reason left him.

He took the knife from his pocket and crept along the end of the bed. As he changed direction and moved towards the man his boot disturbed a loose floorboard, which let out a loud creak. He stopped in his tracks momentarily, but it was too late; he saw the noise had woken up Beth, who opened her eyes and let out a high-pitched shriek of fright.

"Paul! Wake up!"

Edwin's brain raced as he saw Beth shaking the man awake and screaming for help. He made a dive for his bare chest with the knife, but the man was young and too quick. In a second he had thrown himself on top of Beth as the knife plunged harmlessly into the mattress. He saw Beth and the man scramble out of bed and make for the en-suite, slamming the door behind them and bolting it. He could hear them shouting, trying to alert the rest of the family. One of them began banging on the door with something.

He stood by the locked en-suite door, knife in hand. The man would not get out of the bedroom alive; Edwin would see to it. *Beth was his, and would always be his!*

CHAPTER 50

BETH AWOKE AT the sound of hammering and shouting. She got out of bed and put on a dressing gown.

"What's going on?" Liam sat up in bed, rubbing his eyes.

"Something's happening in Amy and Paul's room." She fished around for her slippers.

"Leave them alone. They're young and in love." Liam lay back down on the pillow.

"No, it's not that. Amy sounds as though she's screaming."

She started for the door, but then came face to face with her son in the doorway.

"What's happening, Mum? Joss looked towards the closed bedroom door behind which still came the sound of thumping and muffled shouts.

"Stay here, Beth. I'll go." Liam was at his daughter's bedroom door in seconds.

"Get back! I've got a knife! I've come to take what's rightfully mine!" Edwin brandished the knife, and Liam stepped back into the hallway."

"Who are you? What do you want?" Liam could see nobody in the bed. He took a breath and shouted.

"Amy! Paul! Are you ok?" He could hardly believe what was happening to his family on Christmas Day."

"Dad! We've locked ourselves in the bathroom. Get the police!" Amy's terrified voice came from behind the en-suite bathroom door.

"I'll ring them!" Joss raced back to his bedroom and phoned the emergency services, alerting Toby at the same time, who had fallen asleep listening to music with head-phones on.

The two boys stood behind Liam and Beth at the bedroom door. Joss took a look at the man, who had taken down the hood of his duffel coat and was sweating profusely. He had a feeling a scene like this would have happened sooner or later. He swallowed the lump in his throat and ignored the pound-ing of his heart.

"Hello Dad. It's Joss." He took a step into the bed-room, hearing his mother's gasp of terror coming from be-hind him.

"Get back, you little fucker. I told you before; it's Beth I want, not you."

Joss stood his ground.

"You've got Amy and her fiancée Paul in there, Dad. Mum's out here with me."

For a brief second Edwin looked confused, but then the black eyes glittered.

"You're lying! I saw her with my own eyes! I know Beth's in here!" Edwin gestured with the knife towards the en-suite door. The hammering stopped.

"No, Dad, you're wrong. Amy's not a little girl any more. You haven't seen her since I was born, nearly seven-teen years' ago. She's twenty six today and all grown up. She's getting married next year."

"Shut up! I saw her hair. She's Beth; you can't fool me!" He began to kick at the door to the en-suite. "Come out! Come out now! This has gone on long enough!" He felt sweat dripping down from his forehead with the effort of trying to kick the door in.

Amy screams could be heard again as the door began to give way. With her daughter's cries and the police sirens out-side in her ears, Beth pulled her son back into the hallway, motioning to Toby to turn off the alarm and open the front door. Shaking, she took Joss's place in the bedroom with Liam at her side.

"Edwin, *I'm* Beth. Stop what you're doing and look at me! I'm Beth. Can't you see?" Her legs felt like jelly at the sight of him.

"You're an old woman. There's no way you're Beth!" Edwin ceased kicking and waved the knife around in the air.

"Remember when you brought Amy the book? Re-member when we sat at the table together and ate? You used to bring us sandwiches if you were going out to work and wouldn't be back for a long time. You looked after us, Ed-win. Thank you for looking after us." Beth's voice shook with emotion.

Edwin was silent as he gazed at the woman standing in front of him.

"You brought us a torch in case the light went out. Do you remember, Edwin? And sometimes you'd bring us a new light bulb." Beth moved an inch or so forward, holding onto Liam's hand for support.

Edwin's eyes filled with tears at the precious memories.

"What have you done to your hair? What's he done to you? Let me take you home. You look terrible!" He pointed the knife at Liam, and moved closer.

"It was all such a long time ago. Joss was a baby; he's nearly eighteen now. I'll be fifty four in April, Edwin. We've all changed; your hair's turned grey now too." Beth could hear the police coming upstairs and talking to the boys in the hallway. "Give me the knife, Edwin, and I'll come home with you."

She felt emboldened with the power she had over him. She let go of Liam's hand and moved closer to the madman. She kept her eyes locked on his and saw the knife go slack in his hand. She remembered those chilling beady eyes that used to bore into hers, but suddenly she felt no fear; she was in control.

"Give me the knife, Edwin. We'll miss our train back unless we go home now." She heard the bolt on the en-suite door sliding quietly open, but kept her gaze focused on the man she'd been terrified of for so long. "Put the knife in my hand."

She could smell his sweat. She held out her hand and took the weapon from his unprotesting fingers, all the while keeping her unblinking eyes focused on his.

The en-suite door opened a crack. Paul sidled out, and saw the man and Beth face-to-face, with Beth holding the knife and the man's back towards him. He threw himself at the intruder, pinning him to the ground with the help of Liam and Toby. Beth held the knife tightly and sank down onto the bed in relief, as Amy ran out of the en-suite towards her mother.

Joss looked at his father, overcome and powerless on the floor. The bedroom was suddenly swarming with police. He looked at Liam holding his father down. He felt wretched.

"I'm so sorry, Dad. This has all been my fault. I gave the bastard an idea of where we lived."

"You weren't to know. It was as much my fault as yours; I forgot to lock the garage door, but it's all over now, eh?" Liam smiled at Joss, and suddenly the boy knew that blood was not necessarily thicker than water; he had realised just in the nick of time who his real father was.

EPILOGUE

"HAPPY CHRISTMAS, AND happy birthday Amy!" Liam held his glass of champagne up to his daughter's.

"Happy Christmas Dad, and thanks so much Mum for rescuing us!" Amy clinked her glass against her parents' best lead crystal champagne flutes.

"I don't know if I could ever do anything like that again though. It just seemed the right thing to do at the time." Beth passed around hot plates and tried to put it out of her mind.

"I'd like to give Amy her birthday present now."

Paul took a plate, fished in his pocket for a small wrapped box, put the box on the plate and passed it on to Amy.

"What is it?" Amy smiled and turned the box over in her hands.

"Well, you won't find out unless you open it, eh? Toby laughed.

"Yeah, hurry up; I want to eat my dinner!" Joss looked hungrily at the steaming turkey in the middle of the table.

"You and your stomach." Tara leaned over and gave Joss a kiss on the cheek.

Amy looked quizzically at the contents of the box. "What's the key for?"

"You know that house you said you liked in Bury? Well, you now own half of it. I know I said it was too much money, but then we er…. got a little bit of help as a Christmas present." Paul held up his thumb. "Cheers, Beth and Liam; we couldn't have done it without you!"

Amy stood up from her chair and threw her arms around her parents and then around her fiancée, burying her head in Paul's shoulder as the tears came.

"I don't know what to say!"

"You don't have to say anything." Beth sat back on her chair and grinned, thankful that her family were all together.

"Tara, do you want to pull my cracker?" Toby winked at Tara and lightened the mood.

"No she doesn't. She's only going to pull mine." Joss made a face at his brother.

"I'll pull both of them. How's that?" Tara giggled and reached for the crackers.

"Keep it clean. Keep it clean. This is a family show, eh?" Liam smiled as he began to carve the turkey.

"I don't know what you're talking about Dad, but I'm talking about crackers." Joss reached over and took a spare sliver of meat.

"I heard from the police earlier on that the little black book was very useful to them in finding the main counterfeiters." Liam looked towards Joss. "It seems that there might be a reward coming your way, son. Perhaps your little escapade might bear fruit after all?"

Joss looked up in surprise with a mouthful of turkey. "Wow."

"Is that all you can say?" Beth looked at her son and laughed.

"For the moment. I'm temporarily speechless."

"That makes a change." Tara reached over to Joss and ruffled his hair.

"Let's all have a toast. To family!" Liam stood up and raised his glass in the air.

Beth, Amy, Paul, Toby, Joss and Tara stood up in unison and clinked their glasses together.

"To family!"

Beth looked around at her loved ones and at that moment knew without a doubt that she was the luckiest woman alive.

THE END

If you have enjoyed this story, you may also like 'For the Sake of a Child' by Stevie Turner.

REVIEW OF 'FOR THE SAKE OF A CHILD'

I listened to the audio book of this haunting story about the dark and disturbing world of paedophilia. The narrator, Janine Haynes, had a lovely voice and her narration was well paced and enjoyable.

Ginny Ford is an ordinary and hard working woman. Her loyalties lie with her family comprising of her husband and young daughter. Ginny is a writer of children's literature and supplements her income by working in the early hours of the morning as a cleaner at the offices of PhizzFace Inc.

When Ginny accepts a promotion, cleaning the offices of the directors of the company, she stumbles across information that involves her whole family in the sinister and desperate world of a ring of paedophiles. Ginny and her husband's initial attempts to bring the information to the attention of the local authorities is thwarted by collusion and cover ups at high levels. The couple are faced with a situation where they have to choose between saving their family and taking a significant bribe or pursuing their attempts to incriminate the perpetrators. Their decision has far reaching consequences on the mental well- being of them both, in particular, Ginny, who cannot get the harrowing scenes she has witnessed out of her mind. Ginny feels huge guilt and ultimately is led to making a different choice that puts her family at risk again.

I enjoyed this book and, while it did delve deeply into the dark side of paedophilia and the wickedness of those involved, it also highlighted the goodness of many people and their courage in tackling situations like this. It was vindicating to read about people who are willing to risk a lot to obtain their desired outcome.

OTHER BOOKS BY STEVIE TURNER:

THE PILATES CLASS
FOR THE SAKE OF A CHILD
LILY: A SHORT STORY
NO SEX PLEASE, I'M MENOPAUSAL!
A RATHER UNUSUAL ROMANCE
THE DAUGHTER-IN-LAW SYNDROME
REVENGE
THE NOISE EFFECT: A SHORT STORY
THE DONOR
LIFE: 18 SHORT STORIES
MIND GAMES
REPENT AT LEISURE
A NOVELLA COLLECTION
LEG-LESS AND CHALAZA
A MARRIAGE OF CONVENIENCE